THE

GIANTS OF BASHAN

AMINA HARRISON

THE GIANTS OF BASHAN

AMINA HARRISON

Printed in the United States of America

THE

GIANTS OF BASHAN

AMINA HARRISON

Foreword from the author

Years ago, when I first published The Giants of Bashan, there was a lot of research put into my book, and although my sole intent regarding to the book was to write it fictional, later I found out The Giants of Bashan first draft read like a more historical one. With my personal decision to rewrite my literary baby here, I decided to rearrange the plotting segments also the characterizations, however the most important decision had been left entirely up to me; remove the non-fictional character by the name of Noah. All the same, to keep my writing style of rewriting The Giants of Bashan interesting I kept the backdrops of

the novel in a setting of an ancient land known as Bashan, which in turn I found out was a valley located somewhere in early Mesopotamia, where at one time there were men, who lived in Bashan; "men of renown," because they towered heights, least to be from fourteen to eighteen feet according to historians of the subject of the ancient giants. Also with enough detailing for the ending the deluge supposedly had destroyed the valley of the giants including the entire world.

Amina Harrison

CHAPTER 1

"King Odainat, we have no choice. If we do not move forward with our people, the last of us will die out here in the wilderness," a man of a different valley hundreds of miles from a renown one known as the valley of the giants, is saying a man known as Shullay, the chief adviser to the King Odainat, also it has been the idea of the chief adviser for the King's populace to move away from a region is now dry also becoming desolate because no rain has fallen in the region, one by one King Odainat's people were near the brink of starvation. "Remember, you lost your wife because she has died of dehydration," Shullay says.

"Then gather up the last of our people, the only region we are able to travel is the valley of Bashan, and there, maybe the monarch of the valley of Bashan will allow us to come there to refuge; we have no choice," King Odainat says as he will now goes away to leave his trusted adviser Shullay to gather up the people, to assemble them all as well as the few children, who have died from the oncoming famine to make ready to travel to the valley of the palm, and date trees, livestock a plenty also fresh water brimming from its lakes and streams. Although it is true of what his true adviser had said regarding to the beautiful, loving wife of King Odainat, who is now dead as he is now sitting in his throne room the area of the palace is becoming shabby, and crumbling from its once graceful standing, King Odainat will begin to think about at one time, he was the most powerful king also warrior opposite from the region knew as Bashan. Since those says, King Odainat had believed the valley knew as Bashan must have a peaceful like people, even though King Odainat never did hear or seen the monarch of Bashan, also King Odainat did not have a good reason to battle against the people of the valley of Bashan. Much as King Odainat is aware of the valley of Bashan must have the food aplenty as well as fresh water because one night as King Odainat was sitting outside his crumbling palace, the monarch had seen from afar off a scene of the sky above the region a blazing like red perhaps the people there were having their sacrifices, much like at times King Odainat had partaken in, though not as much because of the oncoming famine happening in the area of where he lives, the people are slowly perishing, and some of his people with the strength they possess were starting to complain to King Odainat. *We have no choice; we have no hope,* King Odainat thinks right now another one of his henchmen are walking into his palace, a man, the king has always trusted one, who has been of sound mind in helping King Odainat create war plans whenever King Odainat would prepare for war most of all for conquest. Lifting his graying head slowly to look at the man, of about the age of thirty even though his muscular body is trying to show a little wearing down because of the oncoming famine in King Odainat's region, the monarch will display now to show to the general of his army the man has the permission to speak.

"Do not feel incapable King, because you along with our people have to travel on the valley of Bashan to survive," the general of the king a man known by the name of Mansour. The general Mansour had plans to marry whenever his king was all finished with his conquering now Mansour has changed his mind with the main concept neither he, nor his new wife would be alive ever to produce children in the near barren region where Mansour lives with his king, and the other almost starving out of existence inhabitants.

"I trust Shullay; we cannot stay here. Tell Shullay; have the everyone ready to travel to the valley of Bashan when the sun god arises the next morning," King Odainat says now he is leaving his throne room and as Mansour shakes his head in pity, in a way Mansour is a little afraid to travel to the valley of Bashan, however the general of King Odainat dare not express if, or not Mansour is afraid to travel to the valley, however it all seem so strange to the general the people, who resides there, not even King

Odainat has the one notion as to really who, or what those populaces living in land thriving with vegetation, cattle, fresh water brimming in streams and lakes nor how friendly or warlike those individuals really are in the *valley of Bashan*.

“Leave them all,” the king’s adviser Shullay says when an old, woman barely able to speak will tell the king’s adviser about the sick, and older ones are not able to travel to the valley of Bashan. Agreeing along with what the king’s adviser Shullay says, the older woman really do not care because of her only living relatives, a son and husband had died in a battle against another tribe of people far away's from where the old woman, and Shullay lives with King Odainat and his populace. As the sun god rises higher, the people of a region not too far from the valley of Bashan will be on their way carrying what little they all have to perhaps be welcomed into a land, though mysterious may welcome King Odainat and his tribe so the people will not in plain sight starve. By the time King Odainat, and his tribe has arrived to the main entrance of the valley of Bashan, the sun god is moving a little lower below the horizon whiles the king, and the others are standing by the wide, and high wooden gate of the valley of Bashan suddenly the wooden gate will open, and out comes one man with what looks to be thirty others having the appearance of King Odainat–of the far, *eastern like* heritage.

"They have arrived high priest Bahina," a man of the valley of Bashan says to one of the high priest of the regions a man almost as renown as the giants a race of men towering between fourteen and eighteen feet in height, who lives in the hilly region of Bashan much like a gargantuan force protecting the valley of Bashan. The high priest knew as Bahina, is also known for choosing certain individuals for human sacrifice mostly ones captured whenever one giant will be confronted by an unsuspecting tribe of people, who have no idea there is giants loving in the flourishing land of Bashan. As he looks at the messenger, Bahina had hoped the people, he had claimed actually existed or one giant the one name Kalev had promised of how he would crush the body of Bahina and feed his remains to the vultures if the high priest was not telling the truth. Also, the high priest of the valley of Bashan hopes if those people, of whom Bahina claims to exist has women also virginal ones, then the high priest will believe not only his life will be spared, however those young, and if virginal women could be used for Bahina's ceremonies to the Moon goddess a celebration when a certain number of men of the valley of Bashan also a specific number of men will meet in the temple on a night of a full moon to relish in each other for sexual, forbidden lusts. What gives Bahina the high priest of Bashan the most pleasure likes during those illicit couplings, is when the men participating would wear grotesque like masks to partner with the women, on some nights when the moon is at its fullest, also the high priest Bahina assumes the Moon goddess is pleased with the tribe of Bashan; on a different night of those orgia's a woman chosen as like a dancer struts, and performs a ritual with a snake followed by the Moon goddess's nights of *whorgies*. Because of his status as high priest to the sun, and moon deities; Bahina when after a moth has passed will summon those women to eat a poisonous, green like apple having the women if pregnant to suffer like a spontaneous miscarriage, for the giants including the high priest Bahina understands now no children are needed in the *valley of the giants*.

"I will go, and meet those people at the gate; open the gate as soon as I have arrived," Bahina says as he will now stand up from a few hours of worshipping the sun god inside the temple made of stacks of bricks, and stones and inside the temple is a stone likes altar, the altar is almost covered with human blood because of the sacrifices were held some months earlier to the sun god. After the messenger has left the high priest, Bahina while thinking of safety than sorry, will before he walks to the gate round up several men to come along with the high priest, even though Bahina also the other tribes of the valley of Bashan solely depends the four giants, who lives way above the hills of the valley as like a fortress as the high priest is leaving the temple of the sun god, he smile with the concept of how the sojourners will take to the idea the valley of Bashan has like an unusual protection for the region; men towering certain heights taller than an average man taller than the high priest Bahina. As he is walking along the dusty, grassy roads like in the area Bahina will shout out also to point out least ten men to come along with him to the wide, tall wooden gate. When one man asks the high priest the reason for the gathering of Bahina with the other men, the high priest will only retort there are guests, who have arrived to the valley of Bashan. "And, only the sun god knows why they have arrived to our valley," Bahina says as he walks carry a tall, staff like pole with a pointed end at the top made of what looks to be iron as the ten men walk with the high priest as soon as Bahina arrives to the tall, fortress like gate of the valley of Bashan, the high priest summons two of the men to open the gate to allow the faction of people, who only the deities of Bashan know why the people have arrived.

“I am KIng Odainat; I come in peace with my people. Where we have moved away, the land is dry and there is no food,” Odainat says as he is bowing his head as if the king is in plain sight begging the high priest.

“My name is Bahina, the high priest of the valley of Bashan. Here, you may reside with us, we claim to be a peaceful group as well,” Bahina says as she looks at the people of the king of Odainat, as he is standing there looking over the tribe of people, the high priest will begin to think also of the new sacrifices will be happening soon when another new moon arises over the valley of plenty of grapevines, food, cattle and streams overflowing with fresh water. Allowing the tribe of King Odainat to come inside the fortress, like wooden gate the king, and his populace is looking in awe at the stone like's buildings almost a little more yet appearing than the house King Odainat, and his society lived in back at their homeland. In a moment, King Odainat and his populace though almost half starving and thirsty will be lead to an area of the valley of Bashan where there is other stone, and clay like houses much like the buildings the king, and his populace had walked by as they are following a man known as Bahina. "You and your kindred could stay here in these houses. You will be given food, and fresh water until work will be found for you. For here in the valley of Bashan, we work for ourselves to take care of ourselves," the high priest Bahina says then now he and the other ten men will leave King Odainat and his tribe to settle into their new, colony like in the valley of Bashan as the king will reminds the few of his populaces to stay close all a sudden, King Odainat will discern his adviser Shullay has a frightened look across his aging, and almost gaunt face because Shullay had almost faced starvation before he had to exodus out with the king, and the others.

The day king Odainat arrived to the valley of Bashan, the high priest when the sun god has fully set; Bahina will hurry to temple of the sun god to light a fire with wood placing it on the altar instead of human flesh to give thanks to the false deity. As he bowed, and muttered a nonsense likes prayer to the sun god, the high priest had seen a few children had came along with Odainat and his caravan as he keep muttering a prayer with no meaning the high priest will have an idea concerning the small one of the tribe of the king. Instead of offering the children as a sacrifice to the sun god, the high priest will allow the children to grow up healthy while too shielding the small ones from the view of the giants, who are living over the hills of Bashan. He also seen there are more females in the group of the children than males and because of the numbers Bahina believes is good, it all the better for what the high priest of the sun god of Bashan has the inside his illicit, and dangerous like brain. As the fire on the stone, like altar is about to become dim, the high priest will stop his praying only to be interrupted by someone else, who has walked into the temple as he adjusts his eyesight to find out, who has walked into the temple of the sun god almost interrupting the high priest he sighs when he sees it is one cow of Bashan. A woman by the name of Liah, a woman, who happens to be the mother of one of those giants of Bashan also Liah is a lover woman to the high priest as she stands inside the temple, the smoldering flames from the fire does not justice to her evil, eyes outlined in charcoal, and right now Bahina observes she is wearing one of her sheer like gowns one Liah usually wears whenever the high priest of the valley of Bashan arrives to her house for a bacchanal night of love.

CHAPTER 2

The day the sojourners from another land had arrived to Bashan a woman by the name of Liah was standing outside her house looking at the to her, starved out group of men, women and *children*. There were other citizens out the day when Odainat and his kindred of people had arrived to the valley of Bashan and they all looked at the almost starved out group of people was lead by the high priest Bahina of whom Liah knows only too well because of the nights of sensual lovemaking Liah, and Bahina enjoys on occasionally certain nights all too frequently. When the unfamiliar tribe of people had walked on to perhaps an area of the valley possibly already sectioned out by Bahina, Liah one of the feverish of the flesh cow's of Bashan had waited until the sun sets then next she will walk to the temple of the sun god of where Liah's lover the high priest likely will be they're perhaps giving thanks to the new, brood of people. Before Liah had set off to the temple, she had put on one of her almost see through gowns and since the townspeople's were in their houses at the time Liah had walked to the temple, she was not shy nor afraid she will be seen despite the facts the people of the valley of Bashan views sex, and lovemaking like the oxygen of planet earth as if all the people of the valley of Bashan needs the sensations of the flesh illicitly than oxygen, and after arriving to the temple Liah had not only seen her lover, she had seen as well he was busy with one of his prayers. Though she too deems her to be a favorite of the high priest, Liah deems her to be almost like the moon goddess ever since she had given birth to a man, who grew up to be taller, and stronger than any other man in the valley of Bashan most of her lover the high priest Bahina.

Since the birth of her giant son Arek, sometimes Liah will use at times her son as like a weapon to frighten some of the citizens of the valley of Bashan at one time, the cow of Bashan Liah had almost eight slave likes citizens in her possession until three of those slaves were used for sacrifices later Liah will have the remaining of those slaves freed. Liah almost takes pride also watching her giant of a son whenever Arek will have an one of those wrestling matches with another one of the towering men of Bashan the giant name Kalev even during those times of watching her son; Liah had often times though her son was trying to kill the other colossal to overtake the entire region of the valley of Bashan, even though the immense area of vineyards by the untold amount of acreage, including the untold number of cattle and streams also rivers of fresh waters, Liah had often times told her son if the towering Arek do have the like idea of overruling the valley of Bashan, the certain region has more than enough for all the giants as well as the populace of people, who lives in the valley.

"Why are you here?" Bahina asks Liah as she walks with a stride to least of all give the high priest a hint perhaps the temple of the sun god wills do for what the cow of Bashan has in her illicit like head.

"Are you not glad to see me?" Liah asks with a laugh may give another one chills by the way it sounds, evil, sensuous and conniving like.

“I am here to pray to the sun god, for our new fortune,” Bahina says right now he has stopped looking at the woman, of whom the high priest occupies his most moments of passion with most of all when after a sacrifice.

“I’ve seen your *new* fortune. Our cattle in the valley is healthier than they, looks,” Liah says as she laughs evener though the sound of her laughter sounds all too evil, she will remove her gown the one almost sheer and now walking closer to the high priest, Liah will kneel down close to Bahina and with her salacious like tongue she will use the organ in her mouth to first kiss the high priest with her tongue in one of his years next moving the organ of her mouth straight to Bahina’s mouth right now Liah will begin to make love to the high priest with her mouth become more than enough for the high priest to lift Liah to place her wanting body on top of the altar after Bahina pushes away the brunt out wood, and next Liah will lift her legs all spread out to allow the high priest to make love to her on the altar of the sun god right in the deity's temple. Lifting up her hips and spread wide open her legs to allow his *boto* to ram, and penetrate deep into Liah's furry, eve's cup of desire until it seems as if she, and her lover high priest will fall out dead off the altar of the sun god all because of the passionate lovemaking the two is enjoying. Though, she has enjoyed the moment of love on the altar of the sun god of the valley of Bashan, if Liah is able to read inside the mind of her lover also know as high priest Bahina, the high priest as he was thumping her wide hips with lovemaking; Liah could have seen the high priest thought all alone of the moment of passion about a young, woman, who had arrived with the group of sojourners earlier.

There goes my beloved son, another woman of the valley of Bashan thinks as she is inside her house looking straight off towards the hilly region of the valley where her almost fourteen feet in height son lives, the lofty one by the name of Kalev. Before the woman by the name of Lyza had gotten up the morning to look towards the hills, she had seen two other persons of the valley of Bashan talking among themselves at the moment, Lyza has asked one, who is a woman about the conversation. "Our high priestess has brought in strangers from a strange land to live among us," the woman though the age of seventy is missing four of her teeth in her mouth sneers as she tells Lyza about the unkempt people, who had walked in with the high priestess Bahina supposedly would be residing at the far region of the valley of Bashan as if those persons were outcasts.

“Enemies suppose?” Is all Lyza asks then now the other woman talking to the older one will says now, those starved out looking persons are deemed as enemies of what the woman knows from her daughter. As she keeps standing in the doorway of her home looking up at the hilly region, Lyza despite the fact her son along with the other giants of Bashan are somewhat feared most of all by the people, who sometimes worships and works according to Lyza's son Kalev, and the other two colossal, however Lyza has plans regarding to her son Kalev. Not only she relishes in the fact of how the giant is feared by most, the mother of the lofty man has plans to make sure Kalev will become the sole ruler of the valley of Bashan also Lyza will be made somewhat as like a queen if all goes well in accordingly. Thinking of the strangers, Lyza will put on her head a hair covering now she will decide to walk up the hilly region to visit her son, who resides in one deep cave located in the hilly region. The cavern is by far the only dwelling large, and spacious enough to house Lyza's son Kalev and also she knows her son partakes of some pleasuring inside his cavern evens if those moments of pleasuring is when Kalev will be entertained by a few women of Bashan, who are dancers most of all for the temples of the sun god, and sun goddess. She is not tired even after walking up the hilly region to locate her son Kalev, as soon as she has arrived to the particular area of the area; Lyza pauses then she smiles because as soon as she has arrived to the steppe, grassy region of the valley of Bashan, the mother of the colossal by the name of Kalev has arrived all in the nick of timing as she sees Kalev is right now in a wrestling match with one other giants, one by the name of Arek. Walking only close enough to not become harmed during the wrestling match, Lyza will sit down only close enough to watch the match, and she hollers out to her son shouting for Kalev to win the match, all a sudden Lyza will have an idea to come into her head. Perhaps her son Kalev will be able to wrestle his way as the sole monarch of the valley of Bashan, and concerning those *foreigners*, who have arrived Lyza senses goose bumps because of the excitement of maybe the way those strangers may act whenever they all lay eyes on Lyza's son the giant known as Kalev. Least of all it will make up for the time when Lyza had lost one of her lovers by a night of a human sacrifice to the moon goddess set forth by the high priest of Bashan, one main one if Lyza's plan goes as; Bahina will be the first the mother of the colossal Kalev will order for her lofty son to kill the high priest by crushing the malevolent man with only one of Kalev's giant, like hands.

I wish now I could lay here and die, another mother of one giant of Bashan thinks as she is now lying still inside her house the one, her dear son built for her all by himself because of his massive size, and strength. The reason the mother of the giant thinks of the like, and sad thoughts are because as she keeps laying in her bed those are the moments the thoughts come into her near graying head, even though the certain mother is only near the age of forty about the time when her son was not only born, and how she had the toughest time of raising the giant also the time when she had met the father of her son Arek. The mother of the giant Arek, will slowly turn over on her cot likes bed and staring up at the ceiling all painted the colors of blues, oranges and reds by slaves working for her son the giant Arek at the time, the mother knew by the name of Jezel will start to grimace because even now if she had the slightest implication of how she will be giving birth to a son, who had grown the height of almost fifteen feet; Jezel would have killed the boy when he as probably only an infant. Still staring up at the ceiling of her house, Jezel will again allow the events of the time when she had met Arek's father one day high on the hills of the valley of Bashan when those days the valley was quiet with seems like the usual people of an ordinary valley working, tending to their cattle and also there were children in those days. Still staring up, Jezel as if it was yesterday was a young woman, all fresh and new to the world, and Jezel had not known any man until one fateful day as she was walking up the hilly terrain of the valley of Bashan and in an instant, Jezel had seen a man. A handsome one, tall though not as tall as his son; suddenly on that day the man had walked up to Jezel admiring her with his blank, yet deep umber like eyes however it was it took for Jezel to believe even at the moment; she had met the one man she could possibly love for her the rest of her natural born life in the valley of Bashan.

She only had introduced, her as she rambled on seemingly to gain the stranger's attention with the deep, umber eyes before Jezel knew what was happening, she will be held ever so tightly to the man followed by her making lover to him and when the moment of felicity was all over;

Jezel had awakened the following morning to see she was all alone where she had met the man with the deep, umber shade eyes. *I must go home,* Jezel had thought on the day of the moment, however she would sometimes go to the hilly area with the hopes of meeting the tall, man with the deep, umber shade eyes, but as the days moved on by; Jezel did not ever see the man again most of all her abdomen had became swollen to the point, Jezel could hardly walk up the hilly region of the valley of Bashan. When the time of the birth of her son Arek arrived, Jezel had the four midwives to help her with the delivery with one of those midwives running out Jezel's house in fright most of all by the size, and the way the baby appeared when after birthing out of his mother's birth canal. "It looks as if the babe is one from a god, we do not know of," the other midwife had exclaimed, and for the remaining of the months; Jezel did not take to the baby too much, also she had wanted to offer him as like a sacrifice, but the like was not going to happen because at the time of Arek's birth, no sacrifices were performed by the then high priest of Bashan. It was on a clear day, when Arek was almost nine years old, and the boy was then almost six feet tall; Jezel had coaxed the nine year old, six feet in height Arek to try the brook located in the hilly region, and as Jezel stood on the banks of the river, she had waited for Arek to drown, yet it had not happened at all. When after the death of the last high priest, another new one will be inducted for the valley of Bashan, and it became the time Jezel had believed Arek could be chosen for a sacrifice, yet it did not happen. For it seems as if the new high priest, Bahina when after he had seen Arek, the high priest had became a little frightened of the boy, who will one day grows up to be another one of those lofty men. Sensing she had enough of the boy, Jezel full of a vat of grapes of the valley of Bashan had tried to whip her son, who was at the time nears the age of fifteen and was towering now over two feet higher than his six feet.

"I AM YOU SON. DARE NOT HARM ME AGAIN," Arek had boomed out loud at his mother, as he held up Jezel as if he would thrash his mother at one of her clay walls of her house, with no other words said, the fifteen year old Arek will travel up the hilly region of the valley of Bashan never to see his mother again. *If only I could die,* Jezel thinks all the time of thinking of the moments she has regretted giving birth to like a colossal son, Jezel had not realized as she lays on her cot, the mother of the giant Arek has soiled and urinated on her cot.

"My king, may I go out to draw water from the well," one woman, who had came along with her king is asking Odainat while he, and Mansour are in the house of stone and clay seemingly the largest one in the region of the valley where Odainat, and his populaces are living also the house serves like a small palace for Odainat, and he looks up at the woman he will nod to give her the go to tend to her chores at the well. The young woman Jotape has been living with Odainat ever since her only two relatives have died from starvation before Jotape arrived with her people and the king to the valley of Bashan. The day before they all left their starving land; Jotape had heard some news about another region not too far from the one she was living in before the famine hit the area a place in abundance of cattle, vineyards and fresh rivers of water. During the early days of Jotape, and her people also the king living in their abundant land, it could not be really true a land exists outside their territory until starvation hit the region and for almost two days and two nights of traveling Jotape, and the others of Odainat's tribe would finally arrive to the land now appears almost too real, yet it is really even to Jotape. As she hurries out of the house of Odainat, the man Jotape also views like a father, and she an adopted daughter since Jotape has no more living relatives; as she walks along the streets of the area of the valley of Bashan, Jotape is in awe of the way the people are tending to their businesses also they all appears not only so healthy, yet the people of the valley of Bashan are the healthiest Jotape has seen. Walking along and looking around her, all a suddenly Jotape will see a man, later she had learned is like a high priest of the valley, and he is walking along with four other men and the high priest and those men are walking to another building a little more elaborately built with stones and clay, also the building is higher than most of the other houses of the valley of Bashan. Right now, Jotape will look around her to make sure no one sees her not even King Odainat, as Jotape will walk likes a distance away following the high priest and the four men as she walks on without possibly being observed, Jotape will stop in her tracks while holding onto her bucket, to see the high priest and the four other men are walking into the much taller like building. When the high priest, and the four men are all inside, Jotape will walk again this time as if she is indeed searching for someone or something, yet as soon as Jotape has walked closer to the building of stones, and clay; she will stop and peer inside to see what is happening. She is almost frozen in her steps as Jotape looks and sees the high priest and the four men are standing around what looks to be like an altar made of stone talking as if all five is conducting some sort of business. At the moment, what will capture the attention of Jotape is the image of a figure too made of clay all round with long, thick spikes jutting from its stony face and its eyes are large with an even more grotesque like mouth all carved on the surface of the image.

"Those strangers, who have arrived; which one you believed will do for the next ceremony?" Jotape will hear one man ask the man, she has learned is the high priest of the valley of Bashan.

"They arrived with comely women; some looks as if they do not know anything regarding to a man with a woman," the high priest Bahina says as he laughs.

"Perhaps, their king the man known as Odainat will help us with which one of those women will do; another season arrives for a ceremony to the sun god," another one of those men says, suddenly as if the high priest and the other four men are discerning someone is watching, they all turn and look at the opening, carved out door of the temple of the sun god yet no one is there.

I wonder what they all meant, Jotape thinks as she is hurrying to find water well for after all she did mentioned to the king she will have to do the chore of gathering water. As she walks along, Jotape feels somewhat like a person of royalty because her delicate feet are covered by a pair of sandals like all crafted by a man of the valley of Bashan, since she and her people are now citizens of the valley one day as Jotape, Odainat and the others of the tribe was talking four women, and two men all arrived carrying the sandals handcrafted out of the dead, cattle's skin of Bashan the sandals with the jeweled like stones were made especially for the woman of Jotape's tribe. "These are gifts for the strangers," one woman said, with a curt like thank you from Odainat, the group was soon on their way as Jotape, Odainat and the others of the tribes admired their gifts of shoes. Walking along, and carrying her water pail, suddenly Jotape will glance up towards the hills not too far from the area of the valley. The hills though not appearing too steep, are a beautiful sight as Jotape looks at the deep, grassy knolls seem to be rolling along the lush landscape of those hills, now Jotape will walk towards the area of the rolling hills with the thought of soon she will be gathering up the fresh pail of water as she walks on seemingly to walk along a trail, the air to Jotape smells a little fresher, and the more Jotape walks she will see beautiful flowers and birds with brightly colored feathers flying above her head. After she has walked up more to the hills, Jotape catches her breath then she sigh keeps looking around her to rest also, Jotape will sit down on the thick, soft grass to think even though she knows she must compete her chore of fetching the pail of water. When after almost ten minutes of Jotape relaxing in the hilly area she will stand up to her feet suddenly Jotape will see a stream flowing with water, and it sounds somewhat melodic as the stream of water moves on its course perhaps to a body of water knew as a river. She will walk slower not to tire herself out too much as soon as Jotape has walked to the stream of water, she kneels down with one of her hands, Jotape dips into the stream and water tastes so sweet. Now, she will take her pail and dip it into the stream of water, with her concentration of gathering up the water in the pail, Jotape will not see she is watched until she looks up from her gathering up the water, right now Jotape will see a shadow of a man, a tall man taller than she has ever seen. Turning around slowly, Jotape will see not too far from where she is crouched near the stream of water is one lofty man staring at Jotape in a curious like way, one giant of Bashan. Without even thinking, Jotape screams as if her life could be in danger, and dropping the pail right into the stream of water, Jotape will run as if her life really depends on what she has seen, a man of a monstrous like height standing not far from where Jotape was near the stream.

"My child; what has happened?" Odainat asks Jotape when after she has ran all the way from the hills of the valley of Bashan, and she is breathless unable to stand as she falls into the arms of the king.

"She looks frightening," Mansour says right now Jotape looks at the two men, and she is sweating profusely pulling away from the arms of the king, she runs to another room as if Jotape is hiding. "May I should go out, and find out what has happened to Jotape," Mansour says with a nod from the king, the general of Odainat with a sword Mansour created from a fraction of steel and a piece of sturdy wood, he will walks out and looks around to find out what on earth could have been so frightening to Jotape. True enough the citizens of the valley of Bashan has been most welcoming, however on the advice as well as the insistence, Mansour has cautioned Odainat as well as the others of the tribe to stay as close to the region of where Odainat, Mansour and the others are now seemingly separated, and living from the people of the valley.

"It was one giant," Mansour hears a woman says, one not of his tribe a good looking one as he stands not too far from where he has gone to find out what has scared Jotape, Mansour looks at the woman somewhat curious like.

"Of what do you speak of–giants?" Mansour asks, and his is now sounding likes he is angry, but the woman will walk closer to talk to the man, she recognizes had arrived with the strangers to her valley of Bashan. As he listens to the woman talks of the lofty men, who live in the hilly regions of Bashan, Mansour as she talks on; will glance up towards those hills the region where the woman points as she tells

Mansour about the giants. "If they are like gods; are you and your people afraid of those giants?" Mansour asks still staring at the woman somewhat angry like even though Mansour is feeling something like pervasive like a sensation he has not discerned regarding to a woman in long time. "What is your name?" He asks, and Mansour does not appear as angry as the woman talks on regarding to the giants of Bashan.

"I am Zebbal, a temple favorite for the sun god, and Moon goddess," Zebbal says at the moment, she has Mansour still puzzled however he will thank Zebbal, and before the sun sets, the general to King Odainat will be on his way walking towards the hills of Bashan the region of where supposedly men known as giants lives there like protectorates of the people of the valley according to Zebbal. Carrying his weapon likes a sword, Mansour thinks about the woman name Zebbal, and if by some chance the general hopes to see the temple favorite of whom she is known as walking with his strength and stride soon Mansour has walked a good ways up the hilly region of Bashan. Standing still with his weapon ready, Mansour glances around him to take note the region is landscaped very beautifully by far the most eye catching more than where Mansour, and his tribe lives as well as other places in the valley. Right now, Mansour with other hand will lift it to his eyes to shade his eyes from the sun as if is setting and more brightly than ever, suddenly the general of Odainat will divert his glancing to see a man tall as the general has ever seen in his entire life, taller than life as Mansour keeps his stance as well as gaze at the lofty man, and not even flinching to move; Mansour keeps his stand as the giant after walking only close enough looks down at the general.

“I AM MANSOUR,” the general shouts out to the lofty man.

“A SLAVE, YOU ARE?” The giant bellows out and right now believes the lofty man voice rings like thunder in the valley of where the lush, green rolling hills.

“NO. I, MY KING AND OUR PEOPLE ARE HERE SO WE WILL NOT DIE,” Mansour bellows out again, though neither the man of a normal like height nor the giant will not move one step as both the giant, and the general of a normal height scrutinizes one another. The lofty man, who is facing one village evens though the giant has not ideation of really, who the small man to him is, the giant facing the general is one known as Kalev, the one Jotape had seen earlier as she was near a stream of water with her pail. Now, Mansour will look at his spear and without a doubt, the general knows because of the giant size of the creature to Mansour the weapon the general has made is no match if the giant will now contest a fight with Mansour. Without even flinching, suddenly the giant known as Kalev, one Mansour and his king will learns of later; will turn and walk away and from the grounding of where the general has met one lofty man of Bashan, Mansour scenes as if the ground where he stands is vibrating as the lofty man walks away until only the top of the giant's head could be seen then finally even the head of the lofty man is invisible. Walking away too now steadily, Mansour will the few steps as he is walking will turn around to make sure the giant is not trailing behind the general, and in the nick of his timing, the sun is starting to set fully as Mansour hurries back to the region of the valley of Bashan where Mansour, and the king Odainat lives like in a segregated way; soon Mansour and his tribe with Odainat will have to meet again to have a discussion about those lofty gods, who lives in those hills of Bashan. By the time Mansour returns to the area where he lives with his tribe, he will learn from King Odainat of how Jotape has gone completely mute.

CHAPTER 3

"Do you have a sacrifice for our Moon goddess?" A woman by the name of Liah asks as she is pouring for a man one known as the high priest of the valley of Bashan another goblet made of hammered iron, full of wine from one vineyard of Bashan. As Bahina is sitting on a sofa likes is only one made of wooden planks covered with furs from animals hunted and used for either food or fur much like Liah has in her home, and Bahina looks at the crude drawings depicted on the walls of Liah's house, though the art shows the images of men, women and animals in the most unusual positions to suggests love between man, and beast like, now Bahina do not want to talk about the new sacrifice one inside the high priest's head is a woman Bahina has been discerning one known by the name of Zebbal, the dancer, who moves her body sensually like as she dances; also Zebbal has become a favorite in the valley of Bashan always chosen to dance either for the giant gods, who lives in the hilly region of Bashan or Zebbal will be chosen to dance either for the sun god, or Moon goddess. As of lately, Zebbal usually will be chosen to perform for more rituals of the Moon goddess, the deity signifies the rituals of *love*.

"There is still time," Bahina says now he has diverted his glances away from the stony, walls of Liah's house as he drinks the goblet of the wine and still not looking at her; Liah will sit down next to her lover one of the most important men of the valley of Bashan all because Bahina was chosen years ago to direct, and conduct human sacrifices to the gods of the valley.

"Do you want to enjoy pleasure with Liah?" The woman asks as she slowly moves her right, hand across the high priest's lap to find Bahina's B*ashanite manhood*. Massaging it slowly to stir up affection in her lover the high priest, even now Bahina cannot resist the moves Liah is making on him, when her massage is over; she will take the goblet away from the high priest now both she, and he will begin to whisper into each other's lip with pervading like kisses as if Liah, and Bahina is trying to smother each other by *lipsining*. For as long she has waited for the times when the high priest comes to her home, Liah knows Bahina usually do not need too much coaxing when regarding to love suddenly with her full, fleshy legs up and wide spread, the high priest will enter her furry, Bashan cow like phudi, during the moment of their heathen like felicity, the high priest thinks of the sensual like dance for the Moon goddess; Zebbal. Though, she is feeling and enjoying the flashy, cunny moment with her high priest, Liah has no idea her lover is actually thinking in terms of another *Bashanite* woman, and only because Liah feeling like a fierce like act of love on the flooring of her house believes if she never, have a moment of the pervading, intimate moment with the priest of the valley of Bashan; Liah may die all because of the lack of the love between she, and Bahina. When their moment of ardella is over, Liah will fall asleep while cradled in the arms of Bahina though now a crescent moon is rising in the skies over the valley of Bashan, and sun is setting a little earlier than usual even though neither of the citizens in the area of Bashan has not idea regarding to the shortened, and longer days also nights as the weather changes in the valley. Seeming as if it almost three hours as she is sleeping, when the time Liah awakes; her high priest lover has gone out of her house, and now pulling up one fur off her sofa made of wood, hewn logs; Liah wraps the animal skin around her body now she will walk nears her door opening it slightly. As she looks down one dirt likes street of Bashan, then down another direction in the second direction; Liah sees the high priest talking the dancer knew as Zebbal, one woman of the valley Liah has often times despised. Standing in her doorway as not to be seen, right now Liah will think Bahina is talking to the dancer regarding to becoming the next sacrifice for the Moon goddess, and on the mere thought; Liah will glance to see a young man indeed a Bashanite of the valley of Bashan.

Motioning the young man to come into her house, he will in a sneaky like way as her high priest lover, the young man do not need any coaxing as he and Liah while on the floor of her house, the out of the blue lover will hoist Liah to turn over to make love from the rear of her full, thermal for too fleshy *hinny*. As the young man rides Liah as if she is one, prize winning cow of Bashan, maybe because of the thought of her lover man the high priest talking to Zebbal had made Liah suddenly choose the younger man to come into her house and make love to Liah in the way the pervading *mang* is doing to Liah now.

"To dance for you my lord," Zebbal says to Bahina as she was returning home followed by Zebbal meeting Bahina even though the dancer has been perceiving the high priest could be more interested in Zebbal more than she imagines. As she listens to Bahina explains according to a group of men, who works for the high priest in for the charting of the stars, and Moon soon it will be the largest of the moon ever to appear in the skies above the valley of Bashan, in truth the dancer really is not hearing Bahina. Even since Zebbal has met one of the strange like men, who has arrived to live in the valley with his people; Zebbal has been not able to think of anything else nor is no one else no matter how it looks as Bahina is talking to the dancer somewhat interested.

"Acktar, one of my astrologers, believes it will be the brightest Moon ever. As if the goddess is indeed pleased with the people of the valley of Bashan," Bahina says then now with perhaps she would be delighted as well as obligated to dance for the goddess considering what leads to the ceremonies usually a lover's bacchanalia.

Though strange as it seems, with Zebbal as one main dancer of the ceremony; she does not participate in those sensual, passion pits of the valley, however since meeting a man known as Mansour, with all hope Zebbal hopes to not only tell the stranger about the ceremony of the *whorgy* moment in the temple of the goddess; Zebbal hopes when after maybe one introduction also invite to the temple of the Moon goddess, the outlander in her curious land will might want to partake of the sammich night having Zebbal as Mansour's lover's feast.

“Three wives of your army is looking after Jotape,” Mansour says when Odainat on a different morning asks about the woman. Ever since Mansour had told King Odainat about the almost too tall men to be actually human on the certain morning the two men will take a chance to go into the valley of where those lofty men live even though Odainat could not understand Jotape after she arrived to the area of where Odainat and his people are living in the valley of Bashan, now Jotape is now completely mute.

"I thought having more of our men to come along," Odainat says as he is looking straight towards the hilly range of where supposedly men, who are deemed as gods in the valley when in due timing the general Mansour and King Odainat will learn during their days and peculiar nights of living in Bashan. Even Odainat is somewhat amazed of how well it looks his people are adjusting to the extraneous region evens though the valley is overflowing with the substances like food, clean water and cattle though King Odainat believes could last his people for almost two lifetimes it makes out to be. Without Mansour knowing, one early morning Odainat had taken it on his initiative to go out and explore the place Bashan as Odainat walked the streets and the sun was rising over the cerulean blue horizon, Odainat had seen the people on about their way men herding the cattle, women carrying huge, jars, and jars perhaps of the wine from the vineyards, however one concept Odainat had discerned there are no children living in Bashan least of all it is the way it looks from the king's eye. Though, there only nine children, who has traveled along with Odainat when he, and his tribe had left their homeland to go to Bashan, as he walks along exploring and speculating; Odainat is grateful soon those nine children will grow up not only healthy, they all will become adults; and with all hopes, the king hopes the women of his tribe will not conceive in the valley of Bashan, and only Odainat understands deep within him; children from his lineage of people may not be safe in Bashan.

“Alone, for now my king. If we need our other men most of all for protection then you, and I will make a plan. Place Shullay to oversee the tribe whiles we are away,” Mansour says next after Odainat appoints Shullay it will be what the king will says will have Shullay a little apprehensive, yet the main servant to the king will not ask no further questions. Now, with the assurance of Shullay to oversee his tribe, Odainat and Mansour will overlook the people of Bashan seemingly going about their business as the king, and his general is walking towards the hilly region of where Mansour had returned to tell Odainat about the lofty men. As the two is walking up the not too steppe hills with the grassy landscaping as both are almost near the radius of the valley evens Odainat will marvel at the landscaping as the king looks at the exotic birds, the thick, leafy trees as Odainat and Mansour walks on the two will come to a nearby stream of fresh water, the several bodies of water in the valley of Bashan as well as in the hilly region of where the giant lives.

"Are those tall men you saw are hiding?" Odainat asks as he keeps looking at the lush, greenish landscaping of the valley suddenly before Mansour will answer suddenly one lofty man of the valley of Bashan, who lives in the hilly region will make his appearance standing almost too tall as if the giant appears to be monstrous like. From afar off, the giant known as Arek had seen the two men walking along, and he knew those men were not sent to the hilly region for a sacrifice, for the high priest of the valley usually informs the giants, Arek, Kalev and the third one know as Jabesh when one man most of all enemies of the valley of the Bashan will be tied, and bound to be ushered to the hilly region to be killed either by Kalev or Jabesh. Perhaps because of the way his mother had treated him maybe because Arek's mother Jezel was afraid of her lofty son, the giant Arek no not partake of the killing of any sacrifice also because of his massive height there is not one man in the valley let alone the high priest Bahina will have the gall, gumption or courage to dispute Arek. When the two men though obvious not sacrifices suddenly the giant Arek will step out seemingly out of nowhere almost startling the two men even though one man, is already aware of the lofty men, who lives in the hilly region of Bashan.

"It is as you said," Odainat says with a little fear in his voice as the giant Arek standing near enough to the two men only looks down at the men, and holding his sword in his right hand the weapon will have to take hundreds of men to carry; Arek the giant of Bashan is not holding the weapon as if he will strike to the two men.

“Stay here my king,” Mansour says as he will now walk towards the giant.

“Do not be a fool of a general. The man with such a height will kill you,” King Odainat says as he grabs the left arm of Mansour as if the king is trying to stop his general.

“Trust me,” is all Mansour says as he will not lose him from his king’s grasp to walk only near enough to talk to the giant.

“WHY HAVE YOU COME TO MY VALLEY,” the giant Arek booms out aloud at the small man standing ever so bravely in Arek's presence an indication the man is not a sacrifice.

"MY KING, AND I COME IN PEACE," Mansour shouts out with the hope the giant hears him, though Mansour the general thinks if he is to die it will be only because Mansour wants to protect Odainat next have the tribe to leave the valley of Bashan.

"I AM AREK, ONE OF THE PROTECTORS OF BASHAN," the giant bellows out, and now with the assurance the lofty man will not murder either Mansour or his king Odainat, right now what the two men will see the lofty man known as Arek of Bashan will kneel down on one his giant, like knees to kneel closer to talk more with the general and for the next twenty minutes of both the lofty, and the general time; Mansour will also learn the giant Arek is not the one Mansour had met sometime earlier. "YOU HAVE MET MY CONTENDER, KALEV," Arek bellows out again as Mansour waits to hear of what a contender is, the general and his king Odainat will listen as Arek the giant explains the giant known as Kalev is the contender of the two lofty men is wrestling matches. "NOW, YOU TWO KNOW OF WHO I AM; LEAVE MY HILLS, UNTIL ONE OF US SUMMONS YOU AGAIN," Arek the giant says now Mansour will agree to leave the giant right now Arek will stand up, and walk away from the two men vibrating the ground the way Mansour had sensed the day he had traveled to the hilly region of the giants the time Mansour had came to the hills all alone.

"We better do as he says," Odainat says as he is now standing nears Mansour watching the lofty man known as Arek disappears behind trees almost as tall as the giant. "When we return, I will warn the people not to ever come to the hills," the king says as he, and Mansour are now walking and leaving the hilly region of Bashan, the main valley of the giants of Bashan.

"What will you tell the people; if they all want to know the reason?" Mansour asks, then now the king will only reply the danger yet what is the reason of the danger. As the two men are nearing back into the valley to return to the area of Bashan where Odainat, and his tribe is sectioned off; Odainat when nighttime falls will gather his tribe in a secret like place of where he, and his people live to tell them of the warning. As Odainat is falling asleep he thinks of the earlier part of the day he had confronted a man, a most extraneous one, also a giant one capable of killing a score of an army of men at the time, Odainat had assumed he would die from a heart attack when his eyes beheld the lofty man, who lives in the hilly region of Bashan. For the remaining of his life, King

Odainat will always live in fear and not because of the giants, but what will have to his tribe if Odainat were to die, and leave his beloved tribe maybe totally defenseless.

On the evening he had visited her house, Bahina had not thought about whom will be the next sacrifice as he was talking to LIah before the high priest of Bashan, and Liah had enjoyed another illicit moment of lovemaking. He knew for a fact, Liah will not ever do to be one sacrifice for the Moon goddess, her body is already showing signs of eating too much of the roasted meat from one cow of Bashan the people of the valley on the instruction of Bahina with eight other men will kill one cow to prepare the animal for a feast before the start of the ceremony to the Moon goddess supposedly prepares the people of the valley of Bashan for fertility even though there are no children living in the valley excepts for the few, who have arrived with a group of strangers from a nearby area seeking refuge as well as food, and fresh water. While sitting in his house as the sun is setting, also while drinking a goblet of his wine specially pressed by certain men with cleaner feet for the high priest, Bahina wishes now he could only be rid of the mother of one giant. When after Liah had given birth to a baby, who had grown to be almost taller than any tree in the valley, sometimes Bahina had wished he had given the orders then to have the giant known as Jabesh, when the lofty man was a somewhat younger, now thinking about Liah and her son one giant, who lives in the hilly region of Bashan; there could have been no way Bahina could have ordered the death of Jabesh for the giant was almost nine feet tall when he was only twenty years older.

Then again, there is the dance maiden; Zebbal, Bahina thinks as he will stand to his feet walk over to where there is three jugs of his wine, lifting one to pour for him one more goblet of the grapes, the thought of choosing the dancer is starting to have Bahina if only Zebbal was right now in his house, he would have her, make the dancer all to him and only maybe the high priest will consider the dancer, with the soft, olive skin pretty like face framed by a thick, mane of auburn shade hair. Standing near the door of his house, Bahina will open the wooden door slightly and see the sun is setting it seems to the high priest faster than Bahina has ever witnessed. *Should I go to the temple of the Moon goddess to pray, for a sign?* He thinks, suddenly Bahina will observe the dancer knew as Zebbal at the far area of the valley talking to one stranger, who has arrived to the valley of

Bahina. Sipping the wine, and keeping his gaze on Zebbal talking to what looks like the man known as Mansour, with his head reeling from the intoxication as Bahina keeps sipping the goblet of wine, right now he will contemplate perhaps he should make the plans to have Zebbal as the next, new sacrifice for the Moon goddess; however the high priest wants to have the dancer maybe the moment with Zebbal could change the salacious thoughts of sacrificing Zebbal could be turned around as Bahina closes the door to his house, and walks to one of the wooden, like chairs he was sitting in the chair handcrafted like most of his furnishings by certain crafts persons of the valley of Bashan. As the quarter Moon arises, the high priest will fall into a drunken stupor because he has drank one jug of his wine, and had started drinking on a second jug.

"I hoped you would come," Zebbal says as she looks at to her one of the most handsome men, she has ever seen even though Zebbal brought up in the valley of Bashan. Ever since she had met one foreigner, a man by the name of Mansour, while in her home; Zebbal the dancer to the Moon goddess has not been able to concentrate on her everyday affairs when she is not dancing for one of the temple ceremonies for the Moon goddess. Now, as he is standing so near Zebbal at one of the water wells as she is drawing her water, even now Zebbal senses she could make love the handsome, bearded general.

"I decided to again, walk around your area," Mansour says, right now he will help Zebbal with the drawing of her water in her wooden jug, after the chore Mansour will walk along with Zebbal, at the moment the general of King

Odainat will learn more about the valley of Bashan. "My king, and I met one of your gods; one of those tall creatures. To tall to discern to be a man," Mansour says.

"They are giants. They protect us from intruders," Zebbal says soon she, and Mansour will be at her home right now the general to Odainat will take note the dusty, streets of the valley is congested with more people hurrying to, and fro to whatever the citizens of Bashan occasionally do every day. "Come inside," Zebbal says at the moment she will observe Mansour has a look across his handsome, bearded face not to even think let alone come into the home of the dancer for whatever the reason. "Do not be afraid," Zebbal says, and now she is not acting so wanting as she usually do whenever Zebbal meets an occasional man of her heritage of the valley of Bashan, who wants to entertain Zebbal after one of those ceremonial dances at the temple of the Moon goddess. "Sit and I will prepare for you a goblet to wine," she says. As Mansour looks around and see what looks to be a bench likes all covered in furs, while sitting down the general will sees Zebbal's house is more elaborate more than the houses Mansour, Odainat also the tribe of Odainat lives in. Zebbal's house has more furnishings, also it looks to have the four rooms carved with stones to accent her house, and as he waits for his goblet of wine from his beautiful, new friend; Mansour will see a room perhaps like a bedroom of sorts. "I inherited this house when my parents died," Zebbal says as she will bring Mansour a goblet of wine, the item is shinier than Mansour has seen than the dishes were given to Mansour and his tribe. Their dishes

Mansour, and tribe uses are made of wood, and dried clay.

"You are alone?" Mansour says while sipping the wine out of the shiny, goblet and while Zebbal is sitting close to the general, Mansour inhales an intoxicating, yet beautiful scent from her body.

"I have my kinsmen here," Zebbal says then now she will stand up, and walk towards a small, like open window as she stares out of the window, Zebbal the dancer to the Moon goddess will slowly, and yet fluidly like talk to the general. "You may find our valley strange, with the giants and all. But, we try to live a peaceful people though our customs are strange as much as you are," she says then now Zebbal will turn around slowly to look at the handsome, bearded general Mansour.

“There is much for me, and my people to learn,” Mansour says as he lifts the goblet to his lips and right now the general is starting to feel a peculiar like sensation as the wine is drifting into his head having him to feel a little sleepy like.

“Come with me on the next full moon,” Zebbal says right now she is sitting closer to the general as Mansour looks at the beautiful , olive skin beauty he is wondering why Zebbal is seeming to plea with the general for whatever the reason. “On the night of the next full moon; a ceremony will happen at the temple of the Moon goddess. On that night you will see one of our favorites of my people, one we enjoy to come together–to praise the Moon goddess,” she says. Before Mansour replies to give Zebbal an answer all a sudden she and the general will hears a commotion outside the house of the dancer.

Hurrying to her door, Zebbal opens the door slightly right now she will see the high priest Bahina running as if his life depends on whatever is happening also Zebbal will see other people of the valley running straight towards the hills of where the giants live.

“What is happening?” Mansour asks as he stands to his feet holding onto the goblet of wine. As he listens perhaps there is something wrong from Zebbal all a sudden one giant is prodding down from the hilly valley carrying his huge, like spear right now Zebbal discerns something has to be wrong for one giant to come prodding down the hill. Pushing Zebbal aside as she is still standing in the doorway, Mansour now has a frown across his handsome, bearded face as the dancer looks up at the general she will now informs Mansour perhaps he should go home, and maybe tomorrow

Zebbal will have the news as of why one giant has come down from the hilly region.

"I am not afraid of those beasts," Mansour says as he keeps looking as if the general will kill the giant as soon as he has walked down closer to the valley.

"Please, you must go. There is only one reason one god has come down. An enemy tribe is trying to invade the valley of Bashan," Zebbal says as Mansour looks down at the auburn haired, beauty as if Zebbal has somewhat lost her reasoning.

CHAPTER 4

"O, the highest of all men in the land. We were summoned to come here to the hills," the high priest Bahina says to one giant one name Arek, as the high priest along with five other men are bowing down to the lofty man. After Bahina and the five other men stand up to face the giant right now they will learn an enemy from another area a few miles away from the valley of Bashan has gathered up a troop of men to come inside Bashan to wage a war.

"YOU WILL GATHER UP MEN TO GO AND FIGHT. THEN, I WILL COME TO FIGHT THE WAR," Arek says his voice booming almost having the high priest and the other five men to in plain sight to run for their lives even though

Bahina as well as the men, who have came along with is aware of the giants even though the high priest has not been too close to the lofty men of the valley of Bashan. With more instructions from Arek the giant for the high priest to appoint the men for war as well as general next Bahina will ask the giant where the battle will be waged. "THERE OVER TO THE FAR SIDE OF THAT HILL," the lofty giant bellows out pointing with his overly, large finger to where the high priest and the army will goes and meet the new enemies, who are now assembling up to meet the army of Bashan. Following the advice of the lofty man Arek, as the high priest and the five other men are walking back to the valley one of those men will suggest to Bahina to seek out several of the new strangers mostly the men to go along with the other men of Bashan to meet at the certain region to battle the enemy supposedly arriving from the far north of Bashan.

"I heard a man by the name of Mansour, who is one foreigner had at one time served the king of the strangers," one man says to Bahina as soon as the high priest arrives back down into the valley he will dismiss the five men until a new morning because the high priest want to go to the temple of the sun god to pray as well as think on what one man had said regarding to a man of the foreigners known as Mansour. After the high priest arrives to the temple, he will walk inside to see at the moment there is a fresh supply of dried wood for the obvious reason knew as an upcoming sacrifice also the high priest has instructed a group of the new tribe of people to always have a fresh supply of dried wood inside both of the temples of the valley of Bashan for the worshipping of the sun god, and the Moon goddess. Walking towards the stone altar right now Bahina will observe the altar also has been cleaned off from the dried blood from the last sacrifice, now he will heap up some of the wood and placing the pieces of wood on the cement likes altar of where above it is a grotesque face of the sun god taking two pieces of that wood, Bahina will rub the pieces together suddenly there will be small flame slowly to ignite burning the pieces of wood. Looking up at the stony, grotesque face of the sun god, its cement likes face surrounded by thick, spokes to show its fake like rays, the high priest Bahina will utter a prayer not only for the safety of the men, of the valley of Bashan, who will be heading off to war, also the high priest hopes the battle will be an easy victory as he mutters his prayers considering it has been a long time since the men of Bashan had gone off to war to protect their, hilly territory of Bashan. As the fires keep kindling, the high priest after he prays will now begin to think about a certain dancer of the ceremonies to the Moon goddess one Bahina hopes to use for the next sacrifice to the goddess. He will also recollect seeing Zebbal talking to one outlander a man known as Mansour, the one mentioned by one the men, who had gone to the hilly region to listen to their instructions from one lofty man of Bashan. *If the dance is in love with the man,* Bahina contemplates soon the fire he has built to the sun god is slowly going out, and after the fire is out, the high priest will push away the debris left behind from the dead wood after he stands up from his prayers. With a serious like look across his now again face for a man not near the age of fifty, the high priest as he is walking out of the temple of the sun god;

right now Bahina thinks the reason the giant known as Arek had walked down into the valley seemingly to warn the people of the Bashan even though the high priest had to go to the hilly region when after learning the reason for the lofty man stomping down into the valley. As he walks on to his house, the high priest Bahina will forgo visiting the woman name Liah, for the high priest will have to think of a way to approach the king of the outlanders one known as Odainat to tell the man one of his men with several others from the tribe of Odainat may be needed as soldiers to go, and fight to protect the valley of Bashan along with one known as Mansour.

"The only way my king will relent; I will have to be the one to lead his men," Mansour says to Bahina one early morning when the high priest had arrived with eight others from the valley to the region of where Mansour lives with his tribe ever since the strangers had arrived to the valley.

“It is an order from one of our lofty men; one, who lives in the hills,” Bahina says to Mansour at the moment, the high priest will sense his skin crawling all over his body also it seems Bahina's skin is a frigid cold the way the man known as Mansour is looking right at the high priest not even flinching.

“And, if my king and I refuse?” Mansour says as he is right now standing near the high priest ready for a confrontation if need one. Thinking of what the tall, bearded man is saying, the high priest will say one reply will have least of all for Mansour to perhaps to take a second thought.

“The giants of the hilly region will banish you, and your king out of Bashan,” the high priest says, now leaving Bahina there with his men; Mansour will walk to the dwelling of where Odainat lives to tell the king about what the high priest of the valley of Bashan has told Mansour regarding to an oncoming war happening soon. Though, it appears as if Mansour will not be walking back to where Bahina is waiting for a reply most of all from the king knew as Odainat, soon Mansour will walk out of the dwelling of the king to met Bahina with a reply. As the high priest listens to the request of the Mansour, not only the general will be overseeing the twenty men only, who will go to the area of where the battle will takes place, however Mansour will learn soon Bahina will have the swords ready to use as weapons. "Fifty of our men. Will make for a good army though we do not know how many are on the sides of the enemy," Bahina says as he turns to walk away it will be what Mansour will say will have the high priest to stop and turn to look at the general.

“The enemy is still outnumbered since one of your giants will be there,” Mansour says even now the high priest believes the general, who has arrived to Bahina's territory knew as the valley of Bashan has met a man, Bahina may have to reckon with while Mansour stays with his tribe, and king Odainat. When the day of the battle arrived the twenty men of king Odainat and the fifty or more of the valley of Bashan all carrying swords lead by Mansour and seven others, who know doubt where appointed by the high priest Bahina. After arriving to the hilly region there waiting for the army is the giant Arek standing not too far from where the men are arriving, as Mansour looks at the lofty man inside the general’s head the giant alone could destroy the enemies, who have gathered at the exact area of where the battle will takes place the enemy from the North have been waiting for the soldiers from the valley of Bashan for two days.

“YOU,” the giant Arek bellows out as he points to Mansour standing at the very front of the army of men. “COMMAND THE MEN TO WALK ONE HILL OVER; THERE IS THE ARMY. BEGIN TO FIGHT SOON I WILL WALK OVER AND FIGHT WITH YOU,” the giant bellows out. Now, Mansour will walk towards the giant Arek leaving the army a little baffled as the general stands close enough to the giant; Mansour will now shout out to the giant the strategy of the battle against the enemy from the North.

“BEFORE THE BATTLE END, I WILL SEND A MAN TO INFORM YOU TO COME AND

FIGHT," Mansour says now with a nod and stepping out of the way and while carrying his gigantic like sword, and shield; Mansour will now command the men to follow another man of Bashan, who was told to the exact of where the enemy is waiting on the other side of one of those hills of the giants. As the battle wages on with Mansour fighting with as much vigor as he had in the past, even as the battle goes on the general will sees the army of men, he and the high priest had assembled the men are right now killed because it looks as if there are more men on the side of the enemies from the northern plains of the valley of Bashan. "AREK," Mansour shouts out as if the giant not only heard the general however the lofty man name Arek will hurry to the battleground as the enemy from the North before either of the soldiers knew to the exact of what is happening, they would not have an one chance to run from the sight of the lofty man with the long, like braided tail of hair streaming down his almost fourteen feet length backside. Stomping, and swinging his sword the enemy will fall down like rabbits from the blows from the giant Arek's sword, with no more men to fight the few are left from the army of the far Northern plain will surrender having Mansour, and the other remaining men of the valley of Bashan to take the surviving men of the army of the north as captives. As Mansour is walking with the captive men and the last survivors of the army of the valley of Bashan, suddenly the general will stop and look back at the lofty man to see the giant known as Arek is walking away from the battlefield with his gigantic sword all bloody over his broad wide, right shoulder disappearing behind a grove of trees a little taller than the giant Arek. Turning not to walk with the men, Mansour will remind one soldier of Bashan the dead must be buried.

“The high priest Bahina will burn the dead as sacrifices to the sun god,” the soldier says having Mansour the general to look a little puzzled. As the army arrives returning to the valley, Mansour and the surviving army will be heralded by the people of the valley of Bashan suddenly the high priest will appear to congratulate the army with the announcement the dead of Bashan must be heaped up from the valley of the giants to be ready to be sacrificed in a bon fire like and burned to the sun god. As Mansour stands and looks at the high priest very puzzled like in a moment the beauty, who is known as one dancer to the Moon goddess will run up to Mansour and hugs the general as if Zebbal had assumed she has lost her love lorn in the battle way beyond one hill of the giants.

"I said a prayer to the sun god for your safe return," Zebbal says as she will hug Mansour again having the general to smile.

"This burning of the dead–," Mansour trails off with to ask more regarding to the strange ritual to the general now Zebbal will tell Mansour the burning of the dead only happens when after a battle saves the populace of Bashan to have to bury graves. Now, hugging Zebbal even though Mansour must return with the remaining men of his tribe to king Odainat to the area of where the general has been living in the valley of Bashan with his people, the high priest Bahina is scrutinizing the pretty dancer and the general, the man almost is by now discerned like a hero from a new battle against the valley of Bashan. As the men, who are the survivors return to their home, and families Mansour will go home to his tribe and king though promising Zebbal soon he will met with her again; in the far distance of the valley of Bashan there is the rumbling sounds of thunder very distant like, yet recognizable. One of those sounds even when heard every so often and the people of the valley of Bashan do not have a discernment of the sounds from the sky evens now the people of the valley of Bashan deems the noise to be perhaps from the sun god either expressing his anger or the god declaring his gratitude.

He should have been killed, one mother of one giant name Arek thinks on the day as she is inside her house one the day of the burning of the dead bodies from a battle happening earlier. The mother name Jezel the mother of the lofty one name Arek, had heard there will be a battle, and her son of whom the mother still despises even though deep inside Jezel is still embarrassed by giving birth to like a son, who had grown up to be taller than usually normal for a man. As she covers her face only standing in the doorway of her house, her frail body leaning on the doorsill of the front of her home, and Jezel's face is covered with a small piece of fur like fabric, so she will not smell the fumes of the dead bodies of the slain soldiers a little ways away from the valley also the temple of the sun god; Jezel has been planning her secret exit out of her life of living in the valley of Bashan. Because of the embarrassment she feels because of the birth of her son the lofty one Arek; when night time falls it is the time when Jezel will go out to the market if one is open and on other nights she walks to one well in Bashan to gather up her water in her rickety, wooden pail. Jezel, if she uses her common sense will understand mainly she has given birth to a son, who is almost deemed like a god of the Bashan, Jezel though is revered like the other mothers of the other two giant; Liah and Lyza. "You have been placed far above; you may have your own servants," the high priest Bahina had said to Jezel one day when the high priest as the sun was setting had met Jezel at one of the water wells in the valley. She did not respond nor shown any emotion on what Bahina had told her now it does not matter to the woman, who is also a mother of one giant, the one; *Arek*. Still standing at the doorsill of her house, Jezel hears the shouts, and carrying on's of the people as the high priest shouts out prayers as the dead bodies of the men of Bashan as well as the strangers of the men are burned in heap of wood one by one sacrifices to a farce god knew as the Sun one made only of concrete. *He should have died,* Jezel keeps thinking now she will walk back into her house to think again of how she will make her exit out of the valley of the Bashan as well away from the giants, who lives in the hills of Bashan most of all her son, the lofty man; *Arek.* Sitting on the bench inside her home, Jezel will look to an area of her house to observe she is soon out of food, and waiting still for not only the sun to set also to go to one market Jezel hopes is still opened, now standing up she will lift one of her baskets from a shelf likes in her house to go to the market and preparing to go out before the sun sets too completely and the ceremonies of burning the heroic dead to the Sun god becomes too rambunctious; as Jezel is walking out of her home to walk to the market if one she is able to find is starting to feel a sense of peace as she walks to market area of the valley of Bashan maybe because the mother of the lofty man Arek; Jezel believes her exit out of the valley of the giants are a certain one to carry out.

Although he had gone to the temple of the Moon goddess, Shullay did not stay too long because the burning of the dead of his people also the people of the valley of Bashan had been more than Shullay could stomach. Ever since Shullay has been living in the valley of the giants, he has not been feeling too well because often times when he eats the food all grown and harvested in the valley, Shullay would always come down with the queasiness evens though one woman of his tribe has been concocting Shullay a medicine likes to take, and the medicine had worked a little while long enough for him to attend the sacrifices of the dead now as he is waking back to the region of where Shullay has been residing his head is starting to pound with pain. He does not harbor any bad feelings towards Odainat because the king had chosen Shullay's only nephew to be chosen to go, and fight in the battle against the northern army some of those captured are now living, and working in the same area of Shullay lives with his tribe. Walking carefully not to fall as he staggers on, suddenly Shullay will see one of those captured men held by five of the men of Bashan, and the captive is fighting with all his might against those five men.

"HOLD STILL YOU CAPTIVE SCUM," one man of Bashan shouts out at the captive even though the captive man has fought off the men to be loosen from the ropes while at the same time the prisoner is fighting off the men of Bashan knocking one of those men to the ground, and knocked out man appears as if he is unconscious. Right now another one man of

Bashan will grab hold onto a whip and start whipping the prisoner in an instant Shullay will intervene to protect the man, and Shullay cannot stand to see the prisoner whipped in the like way.

"Stop it, or you will kill him," Shullay says as the fighting, and the whipping has stopped between the prisoner and the men of Bashan. "What has he done to be treated in this way?" Shullay asks.

"It's none of your business," the man holding the whip says to Shullay.

"It is my business you are beating him like one of your cattle." At the moment, the man with the whip will lift the thing and swings it at Shullay as if the Bashanite is trying to whip Shullay, as Shullay dodges from the blows from the stringy, cow's hide all a sudden Mansour will hurry to the scene in the nick of timing because Shullay has fallen to the ground wringing in pain. As Mansour is trying to defend Shullay and keep the old man from being whipped to death as Mansour struggles with the man of Bashan all a sudden the high priest Bahina will hurry with four other men right now there is a crowd of people gathering around the men, who are fighting each other and an old one is on laid out on the grown with whipped marks on his two forearms.

"WHAT IS HAPPENING HERE?" Bahina shouts out now one man of Bashan explains the first man whipped was acting insubordinate, and next the old man on the ground had tried to defend the captive.

"And, this man Mansour came up to fight," the man says.

"No man has a right to do another one like your men here," Mansour says now the high priest will look at Mansour and the man with the whip all a sudden the high priest Bahina will make an exclamation will almost astound everyone looking at the spectacle.

"You general Mansour, and Tirigan in two days of timing; will go to the hills of where the giant lives. There on the break of the sun god; you will have a combat," the high priest says now Bahina will walk away next Mansour will bend down to help Shullay back to the area of the valley of Bashan so the elderly man will have his wounds look after. While Shullay is inside his house with four women, who are nursing his body and wounds; Mansour will try to explain to Odainat the situation as well as the upcoming duel between Mansour and one man of the valley of Bashan. Before king Odainat responds one woman will walk to the house of where Odainat is talking to the general now the king will give the women the permission to speak.

"Our good king; Shullay wishes to be buried in our homeland," she says suddenly both Odainat and Mansour will hurry to the house of Shullay where the old, man is dying in pain while Shullay breaths in, and out heavily Odainat will instruct Mansour after Shullay's soul has descended from his body, Mansour with eight other men will return to the dry region of where Odainat and his tribe peoples had moved away from there Shullay's body will be buried in peace. "He is afraid of burning his body in a temple," the woman says suddenly all of them will hear Shullay's breath leaves out of his body once, and for all. On the following morning, Mansour will do exactly as Odainat has instructed even though Mansour and the other men of the tribe will wrap, and prepare Shullay's body for burial it will be almost sundown when the men have arrived to their desolate homeland. While there Mansour cannot believe of how even more desolate their homeland has become all the men, who has escorted the body of Shullay back home for burial will hears the mournful sounds of the wind in the region as soon as the burial is complete, and a makeshift like headstone made of actual stone is placed on the grave site of the old man, next Mansour and the other men will be on their way back to the valley of the giants. By the time Mansour, and the other men of his tribe arrives it be soon time for Mansour to go to the hills of where the giants live to prepare for an one on one battle with one other man of the valley of Bashan, the one known as Tirigan, who Mansour now believes is responsible for the death of his dear friend, and one elder of Mansour's tribe; Shullay. At the time Mansour has come to the hilly region, the general will sees two of the lofty men standing somewhat afar off as if the two has been invited and a much further down from where the two giants are, Mansour will see Tirigan with the high priest Bahina, and eight other men of the valley.

"I am here," is all Mansour says right now as he is standing where the high priest and Tirigan also the other men. Now, one man will lift a stick and draw a wide, large circle in the dusty area of the hilly region, and now the high priest will say the instructions regarding to a standoff between the general and Tirigan.

"You two must stay within the circle. Fight until the other one kills the other; then that one will be the victor," Bahina says right now Tirigan and Mansour will step into the wide, large circle and with spears drawn the men will start the battle between the two as it looks as if there will not be a winner, suddenly with a quick aim of his sword, the general Mansour will stab jab Tirigan right into his heart having the Bashanite to tumble down to the ground his body's hemoglobin is spilling right out of his wounded chest. Before the high priest Bahina will shout out the general Mansour as the winner right up in the area of where the two giants have been watching the spectacle, the two lofty men will shout out expressing their grateful for the winner, the general Mansour. As Bahina looks at the two giants cheering for the victor the general, next the high priest will look at Mansour all a sudden the high priest will sense he may have not only a competitor living in the valley of Bashan, the general could be heralded as like the next, new leader for the valley of the giants. Leaving the dead body of Tirigan to retrieve for the next sacrifice, by the time Mansour has arrived to the valley again his tribe will be there cheering Mansour on because they all believe the general had the right to vindicate the death of one of their elders, the man Shullay. Before Mansour goes to the house of king Odainat; he will be met by the dancer knew as Zebbal, and as she kisses Mansour after the tender embrace; he will tell her of how much the general has been waiting to visit Zebbal again.

"All the while you were up in the hills; I prayed to the sun god for your protection," Zebbal says as she hugs the general Mansour and she will follow him back to his region the area known by now as the place of where the *unknown outlanders lives*.

There goes the man, a woman of the tribe of the valley of Bashan thinks as she is sitting outside her house in one of her wood, hewn chairs polished to the perfection because the certain woman of the valley of Bashan has the four slaves to work at her bidding, though none of those slaves belong to the people, who had arrived some time ago. As she fans flies away with a piece of cloth from her face, Lyza, the mother of the giant name Kalev had heard some interesting stories regarding to one of those foreigners by the name of Mansour, who had battled another man of Lyza's tribe also she had heard the general killed his opponent as she keeps looking away down from her house observing Mansour he is right now talking to another woman, who is familiar to Lyza the dancer to the Moon goddess a woman Lyza did not really take note of until now as the mother of the giant Kalev looks as if she is trying to make out what Mansour, and the dancer Zebbal are talking about at the moment. As she exhales, Lyza will recall one of those Bashanite men had came to her house several hours when the sacrifices were over, the high priest Bahina full of the finest wines of the valley of the giants also Lyza was a little full of the brew of Bacchus so full, she had intently invited the high priest into her house to make love to the man, during their moment of lovemaking; Lyza made silly like jokes if her son Kalev would ever catch his dear mother one of those salacious women of Bashan, the giant will certainly kill the high priest Bashan. "Leaving so soon?" She had asked Bahina as he was preparing to go away from her home as the sun was slowly rising above the horizon at the moment looking at the mother of the giant Kalev with his bloodshot eyes, the only reply Bahina replied to Lyza he is leaving her house if her loft son makes a notion to come down from the hilly region of Bashan. As the high priest looking nervous like is hurrying out of her house, she laughed until Lyza believed her illicit insides would fall out only to later fall asleep, and she did not awake almost until the nighttime. Still glancing at the general known as Mansour, Lyza is hopeful she will be able to have different taste of love if she ever has her chance to woo the man into her house, next walking back into her house all a sudden the mother of the giant known as Kalev will have a good idea. She knows soon there will be a new festival to the Moon goddess, and right now she is wondering if the handsome, bearded general will attends the festival. Lyza is also aware those foreigners did not have no desires ever to attend the people of the valley of Bashan's orgies like festivals to Lyza's tribal gods. Then again, there is a first time for everything under the sunny skies of the valley of the giants, right now Lyza will prepare to go up the hilly region to visit her son because soon Kalev will be called out as another contender to wrestle another lofty man, during those games of sorts would give the mother of the giant Kalev; Lyza the greatest pleasure to see the lofty men fight down, and wrestle down with their gigantic arms, and legs flinging in the air until one giant give up having the one standing as the lofty *champion* of the wrestling match.

By the time Lyza arrives to the hilly region she will see her son is drinking one of his many jugs of the wine, as she looks at him drinking Lyza will think of the many times she had warned her beloved, lofty son of whom the entire valley of

Bashan tribe people are really afraid of not to drink too much of the wines of the vineyards of Bashan. After he drinks the last overly, large jug the giant Kalev will glance up to look at his mother as she walks towards her son, who has been born very much taller than the other men of Bashan. "You should not drink too much. You could lose the fight," she says breathing heavily because Lyza is also aware of her impending age having her to become a little tired every time Lyza walks, and climbs up the hilly region to go, and visit her son.

"I DRINK AS MUCH AS I WANT OF MY VINEYARDS," the giant Kalev booms out to his mother and now Lyza will remember her son Kalev has been speaking in the baritone yet boom like voice when the giant was near the age of fifteen then towering almost sixteen feet in height even though now Kalev is only eighteen feet.

"You do not have to tell me your contender. I know you will win my dear son," Lyza says as she is almost straining her neck to look up at her son and now Kalev smiles at his mother one, who had bore him, yet the lovely woman did not ever had hinted or tried to tell the giant Kalev's paternal side of the lofty

"THE MATCH IS ON ANOTHER NEW SUN DAY," the giant says meaning on the following day after the festival to the Moon goddess way up the hilly region of Bashan; Kalev with another giant will have a new wrestling match. As she smiles, and her son the lofty laughs as if he could shake the heavens above, with a nod of her head; Lyza will turn to walk back to the valley of Bashan and prepare for the festival to the Moon goddess. Above all, she does not want really to miss the festival and Lyza hopes to have a chance encounter with one man of the outlanders, who had arrived to the valley of Bashan months earlier.

"We do not ever attend," king Odainat says to Mansour as the general is visiting the king a few hours before the festival of the Moon goddess. Ever since Odainat had arrived to the valley of Bashan as well as taken note of to the king the heathen like ways the people of Bashan lives, and celebrates now king Odainat has forbidden his people to stay clear away from those two temples where the people of the valley worship, stoned faced images.

"Would you like for me to go to the temple of where the festival will takes place?" Mansour asks even though the king really wants the general to go to find out if any of the men will attend the bacchanal ceremony. As Mansour listens to king Odainat as well as the instructions to go, and make sure the men of Odainat's tribe does not partake of the forbidden, lustful ceremonies at the moment, Mansour thinks only of one woman of the valley of Bashan, and the general even now believes he has fallen in love with the one known as one principal dancer to the fake deities; Zebbal. Still listening, however both men will hear something like the sounds of distant thunder a sound Mansour had been told by Zebbal was brought on by the Moon goddess in the skies above the valley of Bashan as a signal the Moon deity is grateful for her faithful tribe of Bashan. "I will go to the temple. If any of our men are there; I will command they return here to our commune," Mansour says now with a nod of approval to go to the festival, before Mansour leaves he will lift his sword to take along with him. Ever since his duel with one man of Bashan, the general always will stay armed, and ready with his iron, and wooden like sword. As he is walking into the far region of the valley, Mansour will see there are now people hurrying to the temple and some of those people act as if they are already drunk with the wines made from the vineyards of Bashan. Regarding to the vineyards now the vines look as if the plants are not growing many full grapes while one day as Mansour along with a few other men were working out in the vineyards, one man had brought to Mansour's attending the ground where the rows, and rows of vineyards grow is becoming a little dry. "Maybe soon the moisture will fall from the skies above the valley," Mansour had said as he was holding some of the dried dirt in his right hand on that day. Before he arrives all the way to the temple,

Mansour will see the young woman he has indeed fallen in love with and she observes the general.

"You have changed your mind to come to our festival?" Zebbal asks the general as Mansour smiles, he will however tell the beauty a simple answer of no.

"My king has instructed me to come, and find out if any men of our tribe will be there at the temple," Mansour says though now he is smelling the intoxicating, flowery perfume likes scent Zebbal is wearing also the general will sees a gown of fur, and silk like draped over her body almost exposing her beautiful, slim *Bashanite* body.

"Come, the festival is about to begin," Zebbal say as she takes his right hand leading the general to the temple of the Moon goddess.

Without thinking also remembering of why he should really be attending in a moment Mansour will be inside the temple where there is small urns illuminating the temple there is the sound of music from wooden instruments like the drums, and flutes also the people are enjoying their dancing and the scent of wine is almost intoxicating in the air to the general. As the revelry continues, the high priest unawares of the people celebrating is now at the stony, like altar right there is a small fire as Bahina lifts his arms he will pray out loud even though the people of the valley of Bashan is ignoring the high priest. After his praying as the flaming lights illuminate the stony, face of the Moon goddess suddenly the high priest will bellow out of the people to prepare for the sacrifice. "Bring her here," Bahina says as he will point his long, staff of wood at Zebbal though she was only planning to dance for the people at the ceremony, not only is Zebbal is surprised she will start to scream and fight the two men, who are trying to in plain sight drag the dancer to the stone, alter where now the fire is starting to rise higher, and higher.

"RELEASE HER, O BAHINA," Mansour shouts out as the people, who are celebrating will suddenly stop in their tracks and look at the general, the handsome, brave like face of Mansour is right now all too familiar to the tribe of the valley of Bashan.

"You dare defy the sacrifice of the Moon goddess?" The high priest says to Mansour by now the general is close enough to the two men, Bahina and the struggling Zebbal.

"You Moon goddess cannot see. Zebbal is to become one of my tribe's people," Mansour says then now there is complete silence in the temple of the goddess. Bahina cannot believe of how defiant the general is acting even though the high priest does not want to challenge Mansour to any combative fights now he will motion for the men to release Zebbal.

"So, you want to go, and live with one foreigner the high priest asks, now Zebbal will look at the general very lovingly and she will say her answer of yes.

"But, before I go to enjoin with my Mansour; I want to dance to him, and the Moon goddess for our fertility of love forever," Zebbal says again the high priest will motion for the people, the general and the two men, who were holding onto the dancer to move back away so the dancer will start her *beguine* to the Moon goddess, and a man, Zebbal will go away to live with had forgone her native people of the valley of Bashan. The eight men with the eight flutes of different lengths to give out a different like tune will begins to play now Zebbal will begin her slow, seductive like dance. As the flutes play one, Mansour keeps his eyes on the woman, he has indeed saved from being sacrificed and he did not want to witness Zebbal killed only because of the ceremony. The crowd of the people in the temple is becoming excited as Zebbal gyrates her hips, and sways her arms rhythmically to the sounds of the eight flutes as she dances more, and more the drunken Bashanite are about to tumble down the temple despite the building is made of hundreds of stones with cement like clay. Amid the roaring crowd of worshippers of the Moon goddess, Zebbal will finish her dance next she walks over to where the general Mansour was standing admiring the dancing of his now espouse. At the moment, she kisses him and the crowd of the Bashanite are about to riot out the temple evens though the high priest Bahina is trying to calm down the worshippers yet not even the high priest is able to control the Bashanite's also because of the last dance of Zebbal, as well as the general known as Mansour made an announcement before the evening is over, Bahina will be knocked down to the dirt grounding of the temple because the worshippers of the Moon goddess has become extremely volatile like. Reaching for her right hand, Mansour is leading his new *wife* out of the temple to return to the general's commune as the two is walking and the full Moon has arisen higher over the valley of the giants, Mansour has forgotten to do as his kind had commanded regarding to spying at the ceremony to find out if any of the men of Odainat's tribe was at the festivities.

“Becoming the one for me for the rest of your life; you will have to live as my people lives,” Mansour says right now he and Zebbal have stopped along the way before the two returns to the general’s area of where he lives.

“No more sacrifices. No more dances. I will live with you and your people because we are one,” Zebbal says as she and the general whispers softly into each other mouths because of the pervading caress of Zebbal, and Mansour's lip to each other’s. All during the moment of the hugging, and palpating the full Moon’s rays are shining a silvery like radiance on the general Mansour and his new espouse the at one time, famous dancer of the valley of Bashan to the Moon goddess; *Zebbal.*

CHAPTER 5

The Rains will come--

"You brought one of their women here?" Odainat asks Mansour the following morning when the general after attending one of those ceremonies to the Moon goddess at the temple, at the moment Zebbal is resting in one house of the commune until the moment arrives for not only Odainat to approve the marriage of Zebbal and Mansour, the two wills have their own house to live.

"The high priest had chosen her to be killed to one of their gods," Mansour says as he looks at his king, the man is now ageing somewhat rapidly even now Odainat needs the assistance of either Mansour and one other man or two others also his sight is slowly declining. As Mansour looks at Odainat besides wanting to enjoin his wife Zebbal, the general knows when the time arrives for the king's death, surely Odainat wants to be buried in the area of where Shullay was taken to be interred because ever since king Odainat came to the valley of Bashan with his tribe, Odainat thought the valley of the giants are heavily vegetated and more cattle with fresh water, the king deems the land of the giants to be somewhat a crushed area of terrain.

"Now, go to be with her. Surely the women of our tribe will welcome her; Mansour. I will prepare to rest," Odainat says and although the general made ready to help the king suddenly two other youths the young men, who had been teenagers when Odainat arrived with his tribe and the two, young men will help the king to a room of Odainat house followed by Odainat will rest as well attended by three women of the tribe, non though who are married or enslaved to look after the aging Odainat. When after the king has walked to a room to rest of his house, Mansour will prepare to go to the hilly region of where the giant lives, and although he had promised Zebbal of how the general wills join his wife later, Mansour has became a little interested in the wrestling matches between the three giants of the valley of Bashan. Before he walks out of the king's house suddenly a woman of the general's tribe will met Mansour and what she says will astound Mansour. "I wish to go to the hills with you," the wide-eyed woman says though the general wants to protest, Mansour will go ahead and allow the woman to go with him to the hilly area as the two walks along, Mansour is surprised the woman has been waiting to go up the hills to attend one of those wrestling matches. Without even her king knowing, the woman knew as Measa had visited the hills of where men she had heard the general Mansour and Odainat talk about men, who are taller than any others who lives in the valley, men, who seemed unreal the naked eyes of all the people of the valley of Bashan, also want ups Measa's curiosity is those lofty men are revered as gods, and guardians of the people of the valley. The sun was setting though not too far down the horizon the day when Measa had gone to the hills to have a look sees at one of those giants, and when she arrived; Measa had seen one with long, reddish like hair tied behind overly, wide backside accenting his even giant like arms, and his legs look like gold like towers to Measa even at that moment she had fallen in love with the lofty known as Arek. She stood still as the giant was drinking out of one those wide, rivers of the hilly region and when he had stood up slightly the lofty man name Arek only smiled at the woman, at the time Measa could not understand why even those Bashanite's of the valley acted so frighten regarding to the giants of Bashan. She held her breath, also her heart beating fast as the giant looking at Measa still smiling somewhat slightly before he would turn and walk away his towering, muscular body disappearing behind a grove of trees the giant is either taller than some of those trees, and some shorter than Arek, yet one day as Measa was in the market place she had overheard one of those Bashanite women talks of a match a fight likes happening between the giants. As Measa stood close enough listening, she had almost forgotten why she had came to the market, however the news of a match of the giants had aroused her curiosity until the opportune moment arrives for Measa. Now, she is walking up the hilly terrain with the general of her tribe, Mansour, who the other Bashanite are about to reverence the general ever since Mansour has been standing up against the high priest of Bashan, and one Measa hopes will one day be destroyed either by Mansour or one of those lofty like men.

“I am sure our king will not be angry. For I am coming along with you,” Measa says as she keeps walking alongside the general, however Measa will not bring up the subject of Mansour's new wife, one of the Bashanite women, who Measa has the distinct discernment, the outside woman of the valley of

Bashan may be ostracized by Measa, and Mansour's tribe.

"Yes, stay close. It could be danger up there today," is all Mansour says soon both the general and the over curious woman Measa will be arriving to the hilly region where there is other Bashanite's obviously there to see the wrestling match between the giants. Still standing closes to the general, Measa will see she and Mansour are standing close to observe the wrestling match in a moment two of those giants, one Measa had seen earlier and another one his hair all over his overly, large head in curls like pulled away from his giant like face with a huge, leather band. Watching ever so closely as Measa stays closer to the general, it will be the giant with the overly, large curly hair will call out the one Measa had seen, the lofty one named Arek.

“TODAY OF ALL DAYS ,” the lofty one says to the one name Arek as the two giants are almost standing face to face to begin a march of wrestling.

“THERE COULD BE ONLY ONE VICTOR; KALEV,” Arek booms out now the two giants are walking in a circle preparing to fight one another.

“SO BE IT AREK; SO BE IT,” the lofty one name Kalev says suddenly the two giants will grab a hold of one another as the cool winds blow in the hilly region of Bashan, the two lofty men Arek and Kalev will tussle, and grab also fling each other all over the space of the hilly region wrestling like two, oversized bulls amid the shouts, and screams of the Bashanite, who have arrived to the hilly area to watch the match. “KILL KALEV,” one woman of the valley screams out the woman, who is the mother of the lofty man, Kalev. As she laughs, and shouts out with to cheer her giant like son to win the match, Lyza wanting to take her mind off the sacrificial ceremony sometime ago, has eased her feelings off another Bashanite woman, who has been saved by one foreigner of the tribe of people, who has sought refuge in the valley of Bashan. Before she shouts out to her son, Lyza will glance up and take note of the general she had seen, and be sensing some pervading feelings towards, the mother of the lofty man Kalev is almost again curious of whom the young woman is with the general at the wrestling match. *Did he not change his mind not to love Zebbal the dancer?* Lyza thinks and averting her glance away from the general Mansour the strange like woman, Lyza will see her son has Arek on the ground the lofty man is trying to lift his body to defend and finish wrestling against her son Kalev then now the match will takes a different turn. Suddenly, the giant Arek will lift his body to toss Kalev completely off Arek's broad one, and next the two giants will continue to fight, and wrestle right now Kalev will do something a little crooked like. The giant Kalev will take out a knife, and lugging it towards Arek missing the lofty man by an inch evens though the knife will grazes Arek's right, broad and giant like arm; lifting his left, feet as giant like as his body, the lofty man Arek will kick the knife out of Kalev's hand to continue the fight the lofty opponent knocking Kalev to the ground.

“GIVE UP OR DIE, YOU FOOL,” Arek the lofty man says to his opponent Kalev the giant, and all a sudden Kalev will bolt up from the grounding to charge at Arek, knocking Arek down again the two lofty men will wrestle each other again as the crowd of the Bashanite's are overcome with more shouts, and screams during the wrestling match.

"DARE YOU CALL MY SON; FOOL," Lyza shouts as she runs nearer to the arena likes to scream at Arek for the insults he has shouted at her giant of a son, however Lyza should have kept her distance away from the two giants wrestling. Suddenly as Arek lifts the giant Kalev to throw him down on the ground plainly to end the match, with all his might as he lift Kalev then tossing him the lofty giant will land right square on his mother crushing the haughty mother of the giant Kalev's to death when Kalev lands on his mother from the toss from Arek. At the moment, there is a stillness as well as quietness as the towering Kalev will lift his body and see the crushed one of his mother, and now letting out a wail ringing the entire hilly region as well as the valley of Bashan, with his seemingly failing strength he has left from the wrestling match, Kalev holds the crushed body of his mother now falling down to his knees it looks as if the giant is in deep sorrow for the accidental death of his mother. Sensing now a little pity, the lofty giant known as Arek with his bleeding, right arm will walk away from the match leaving Kalev still holding his dead mother, and the Bashanite, who had came to the wrestling match will remains still to wait, for the defeated, gargantuan Kalev to place his mother down, and on the instructions of the high priest Bahina, maybe Lyza's body will be used for a new sacrifice for one god of Bashan. As times passes, it seems like hours before Kalev will place his mother down gently on the ground, and next the giant will silently walk to his cave leaving the Bashanite's a little dumbfounded and most of all afraid, because none of the people of the valley of Bashan has not ideation of what the lofty man Kalev will do because of the tragedy of his mother. When Kalev is no longer in sight, four of the men will go to where Lyza's crushed body is and will lift it to carry it back to the valley. As the Bashanite are filing out of the hilly region, Mansour and Measa will follow along later even now as she walks alongside the general, of what Measa has witnessed a wrestling match between the two lofty men, her curiosity, and her desire has become over flamed with passion because the one colossal Measa had wished to win did despite the tragedy Measa had witnessed at the match between the giants. Though, she had heard her son Arek will be contender again in another wrestling match, one that day Jezel did attend however she also had made the plans to finally she believes to come to rest regarding to her lofty son, one of whom Jezel had sometimes abused a little badly until Arek became older and much taller than his mother plainly to defend himself. After she had watched the defeated colossal, the one, who had lost the wrestling match against her son; Jezel did not return to the valley of Bashan with her other tribe. Instead she had walked in an opposite direction until Jezel had found one of those lakes one larger than the other bodies of water next removing her clothes though she cannot swim, Jezel had leaped into the lake allowing the currents underneath to sweep her body farther, and farther away until Jezel could not keep her head afloat above the water next her body will submerges deeper, and deeper until her lungs became too full of the water to hold any more oxygen. Though, no other Bashanite had seen Jezel walking in an opposite direction to one larger lake of the hilly region as her body underneath the water floats on, and on it will not be long before Jezel's swollen, dead body will be drifting out towards the Mediterranean sea because of the currents underneath the lake where she had jumped in to kill herself.

I go now, I will return before the sun sets, Measa thinks as she is gathering up a bag of herbs, her tribe uses to heal their bodies ever since Measa along with king Odainat also the others have sought refuge in the valley of Bashan to ease their bodies of sickness, and injuries. She is ever so grateful; Measa was able to see one of those wrestling matches between two giants of Bashan. Walking out of her house, one she shares with her only brother, and older sister as she is also leaving the house to walk to the hilly region; Measa will look both ways of her as she hurries to the region of where the giants reverence as gods supposedly lives. She is surprised as she walks Measa is not at all tired, as she walks on up the hilly region, she will stop suddenly at the moment, Measa will observe the lofty man, who had won; Arek the colossal is again at the area of where the match had taken place earlier. Measa holds her breath as she walks cautiously towards the giant, even though she sees he is sitting his massive body appearing even lovelier to average in height woman, also the lofty one Arek looks as if he is deep thought. Before she walks closer to the giant Arek, Measa will pause right now he lift his broad, giant though handsome head to look at Measa. *Odd, yet I see such pity in his eyes,* Measa thinks now walking closer to the lofty man all sudden Measa is not afraid of the colossal, also she observes his injured arm still looks the same.

"Pardon one, I brought herbs to heal your arm," Measa says now she is close enough to see the extraneous man of such a height all uncommon though, and as Arek looks at the woman as if the giant knows the woman has feeling for him all about love, he will move his injured arm low enough for Measa to take care of it because the cut is at the lower part of his massive, bulky arm. Taking out the medicinal herbs, Measa will rub the giant's injured right arm, and now Arek will smile slightly despite the tragedy happened between he, and another fellow lofty man.

"You are not afraid?" Arek asks Measa now, his voice does not sound like an echoing boom.

"My king taught me, and my people; fear eats away the soul and mind," Measa says as she keeps rubbing the salve of medicinal herbs on the bulky, like right arm of the giant. "There. Maybe tomorrow; your arm will be much better.

I will return to your hills again, if you like," Measa says as she looks almost into the eyes of the lofty man maybe because of the love Measa is sensing by her admiration of the giant, there is like a handsome sort of tenderness about the winner of the wrestling match. Nodding to show a yes, the lofty man Arek will slowly stand to his feet and turn to walk away from Measa as she looks lovingly at the giant until he disappears behinds the tall, thick like trees. Gathering up her bag of medicinal of herbs, suddenly Measa will hear the thrum likes sounds from the skies above the hilly region turning around to hurry back to the commune of where she lives with her tribe in the valley of Bashan, the sound of the thunder is about to frighten Measa because of all the years she has lived in her territory before arriving to the valley of plenty with her king, also the others of the tribe; Measa has never heard the like sound coming from the skies above as she hurries back to her commune, it sounds like the muffled, like yet rumble sounds are approaching right behind Measa.

"You know what to do," Odainat says between breaths of air as he is lying out a fur likes bedding because the at one time king of his tribe is now slowly dying. Odainat knew in time he will be not only returning to; he also knew it would have to take death for the king evens though all the time of Odainat and his tribe living in the valley of Bashan, the king had thought of leaving the valley after finding out the heathen like ways of the people of the valley, yet he knew now not one of his kin's people would now want to land. The man, Odainat is talking to, who is leaning down close to him on his knees are Mansour, who has by now became almost as infamous as the lofty like men of Bashan since Odainat has rescued a young woman of the valley, as well as defended the now dead Shullay from being whipped alive before Shullay had died with a slight nod of his head, suddenly the last of King Odainat's breath is now gone out of his body.

"We have much to do," Mansour says to another man, who is also in the house of the now dead king, who had ruled with dignity and respect in his land until famine had came down on the area of where Odainat lived with his tribe, and as the man is leaving the house of Odainat still kneeling down to the dead king on a mat covered with the animal furs of the cattle of the valley of Bashan, the general, who had been brought up to serve King Odainat during the earlier years will shed one, lone tear right now Mansour's new wife will walk into the house evens now Zebbal is able to discern the king, she had met is now dead. The way her husband Mansour's tribe views and accepts death is totally different from the way Zebbal's people of the valley of Bashan views the time when a person expires. All her years of living in the valley whenever someone dies in the region of the giants there will surely a sacrifice to one god of Bashan ether the sun one or the Moon goddess. Sensing his wife is in the house of the dead king Odainat, Mansour will stand to his feet and face her also he is not angry his wife has come inside the man the general Mansour had almost deemed like a father as well is what Mansour had told Zebbal the first week she has been living in the commune of the foreigners with her husband Mansour. As he will hold her after Zebbal walks to him, the general will now explain in two days of timing Mansour must return to his land to bury the king Odainat later he will be returning home to the valley of Bashan.

“I must travel with you,” Zebbal says as she is now looking into the eyes of the one man, who not only saved her from a senseless sacrifice, yet the general Mansour is the only one she truly loves also since her marriage to the outlander, Zebbal will kill for Mansour if she has to if to preserve the love between the at one time dancer, and the general of the now dead king Odainat.

“Stay here with my people. Need not to worry. I will return as soon as my king is buried into his beloved homeland,” the general Mansour says and on the same night as four men are in the house of King Odainat back in their humbled house Mansour, and Zebbal will make love as if the two believes the general may not ever return to the valley of Bashan ever again, yet the at one time dancer will believes if she has to pray to one of her gods for his safety, so shall Zebbal *pray*.

"They are now gone, high priest," another Bashanite is saying to the high priest Bahina one morning when the high priest had called an assembly of other men of the valley of Bashan to meet Bahina at the temple of the sun god to discuss the business of finding a way to be rid of the general known as Mansour. Ever since the general has shown his display of bravery most of all by visiting the hilly region of the giants also defending one of his tribesmen; Bahina has been thinking of an insurrection against the general Mansour because the high priest believes the general is gaining more trust in him than Bahina is able to keep it for the Bashanite for obvious reasons. As he looks at the messenger, who has been spying on the house of where the general lives with one woman of Bashan for several days, now with the assembly of men, the high priest will learn the general Mansour is now on his way back to his homeland for a burial of the king Odainat. "We could attack his commune, while Mansour is away," the messenger suggests amid the murmurs of the assembly of the men gathered at the temple of the sun god as Bahina looks at the messenger and despite the suggestion right now the high priest believes to attack the commune at the far area of the valley may not be a good advice.

"That will not be too wise. We must give Mansour enough time to gather up enough of the men of his tribe then we will all meet at the region of where the giants are–next strike,"

Bahina says as he looks at the meeting of the men look to be almost twenty.

"What of the giants?" Another one man at the gathering in the temple of the sun god asks, now Bahina will have the answer evens though he had thought about bringing in the giants as extra militia.

"There might not be a need," the high priest says now the assemblage of men will talk more of not only bringing a certain number of men together to war against the general Mansour, however Bahina will also instruct the messenger to hurry to the iron smith. "We will need more swords," is all the high priest says then now the messenger will be on his way to the only iron smith of the valley of Bashan. Though, Bahina believes of how he may set up the instrumental like plan to kill the general Mansour, and take over the commune of his people; one aspect the high priest had overlooked. In the assembly of the men there will be one traitor all because he believes the high priest is becoming too hungry for power also the one man assumes Bahina has became obsessed with sacrificing the dead of the valley of Bashan, also the region is about to become a little drier than usual because rain has not fallen in several months somewhat blaming the blood thirsty, high priest for the reason of the scarceness of rain.

After four days of timing, the general Mansour will be returning to the valley with the entourage of men, he had taken along with him also the burial of king Odainat is now finished, the soul of the at one time, wise king of his domain outside the valley of the giants had ruled is now resting peacefully. As soon as Mansour has walked in the gates of the valley, he will see a group of men standing with the high priest and what astounds the general the group of men looks like an army. Motioning for the men, who had traveled with him to stop at the moment the high priest Bahina will shout out the reason for meeting Mansour also the general will observes the high priest and his army of men are all armed.

“You desire a war?” Mansour shouts at the high priest and now as he waits for an answer, there in the distant of the skies above the valley of Bashan is the rumble likes sound in the clouds.

“We are here to fight for our land of Bashan,” the high priest says.

“None of my people have wanted your land. You welcomed us as sojourners.”

“The gods of our land is not pleased. You and your men must prepare to fight,” Bahina says then now all a sudden the traitor, who was at the temple of the sun god, will appears breaking between the high priest and his so called army Bahina has gathered.

“GENERAL MANSOUR, THE PEOPLE OF THE BASHAN DOES NOT WANT A WAR. THEY WANT YOU TO RULE OVER US ALL,” the man shouts out all a sudden before he will speak out again, Bahina the high priest of the valley will strike the man with his sword killing him in front of all the men of both sides.

“If you do not want no more bloodshed, you and I will fight,” Mansour says right now some of the men of the high priest’s army had a now backed away. “Meet me up at the hills of the valley of the giants,” is all general Mansour says to the high priest later the two men will be at the hilly region, and the area is quiet since the day one of the lofty men’s mother had been crushed to death by her son during one of the wrestling matches. As Mansour, and the high priest prepares to fight some of the Bashanite, and the people of Mansour's commune have gathered up at the hilly region now with both men holding drew swords, the general Mansour will first strike with his sword now seems like almost thirty minutes the high priest and the general of a long ago king will fight with the their swords. Before Bahina will lift his swords, the general Mansour will strike the high priest knocking him on the ground because the left shoulder of the high priest is bleeding from Mansour's sword. "KILL, KILL, KILL," mostly the people of the valley of Bashan is shouting out as Bahina is laid on the ground holding his bleeding shoulder.

"Your people have decided," Mansour says as he will now lift his sword, but before strikes the injured high priest, Mansour's lovely wife Zebbal will hurry to her husband with tears welled up in her dove likes eyes. “The high priest here, before you came to live with my people; have cause much grief by his blood thirsty sacrifices,” Zebbal says.

“You wish him to live?” Mansour looks at his beautiful wife, now without a word from her; Zebbal will take the sword from her husband next with one swift blow also all her might, the at one time dancer to the gods of the valley of Bashan will behead the high priest Bahina. Amid the shouts from the people, now it looks as if the general Mansour and his wife Zebbal have a now been placed as the new monarchs of the valley a move the area of the giants have not had in years of long ago; only at one time the dead, and headless body of the high priest Bahina on the ground had acted as the one, true leader of the valley of Bashan. Instead of a blood sacrifice of the dead priest, the headless body of Bahina will remain on the hilly, plain like area of where he died to be plucked by the vultures of the region of Bashan until there is nothing else of the dead priest not even the eyeballs of his head the organs too eaten out by the vultures.

Standing only a far away, the lofty one name Jabesh had seen the people from the valley gathered up perhaps for another fight and when it was all over the giant had seen one dead, headless man on the ground bleeding from a sword fight with another man of the valley. Though, the lofty one Jabesh did not partake up in the wrestling matches between he, and the other two giant, ever since he had grown to like a towering height, Jabesh has been placed as like a human watch tower over the hilly region as well as the valley of Bashan looking out for any approaching enemies towards the two regions. When after the people of the valley had all gone, Jabesh will walk out from behind his fortress likes place to observe the dead man even closer right now the body is all too familiar to the lofty man. Whenever his mother Liah would come to the hilly region to visit, and talk to her giant like son Jabesh, his mother Liah often would talk of the way the now dead, high priest Bahina has been acting to have the people of the valley of Bashan to live in fear of the high priest, however Liah knew to omit any details of how she has been a lover to the high priest to her son, Jabesh. Now, walking away from the dead body because there is a circle of vultures overhead waiting to land on the carcass of Bahina, the lofty one name Jabesh will walk to the cavern of where another giant lives, and has been staying like a hermit ever since the giant name Kalev had killed his mother it seems by accident. After walking to the cavern, Jabesh will peek inside the dwelling now Jabesh will observe the giant Kalev is laying flat on his back as if the lofty man is dead like the high priest. As Jabesh keeps watching from the very, wide opening to the cavern, the lofty Jabesh will make out it looks as if the giant Kalev is still breathing, and alive even though from looking inside Jabesh sees Kalev's is starving and wasting away. He will not call out to the giant inside his cavern, however the lofty one name Jabesh will observe something else peculiar like on the body of the lofty one name Kalev. Right alongside of both of the legs of Kalev, are big, reddish pot marks oozing with a thick, liquid like fluid. Though, the lofty one Jabesh has not ideation soon the entire hilly region as well as the valley of Bashan will be struck with a disease likes small pots, now Jabesh will stop looking in on the giant Kalev, next Jabesh will walk back to his cavern, his dwelling is not as gigantic like the one Kalev lives. Before Jabesh will return to his cave likes dwelling all a sudden the lofty man wills see the third giant Arek, the one who had a wrestling match against Kalev. As Arek is walking closer, and closer to Jabesh, the colossal is staggering as if Arek has been drinking too much of the wines of Bashan. All a sudden, right before the eyes of the giant Jabesh, the giant Arek will collapse on the grounding right in front of Jabesh, though not too close the handsome face of the lofty one name Arek is covered with the reddish, pot marks the sores also easing out with pulse like fluid, also Arek is laboring with breathing as the towering man is laid out on the ground.

“Our general Mansour, there are more people who are now in the lakes for our cattle,” one man, who has been busy reporting the outcome of the sick people of Bashan and although it looks as if there is not many soon the entire valley will be affected, so to the point the general now turned monarch of the valley of Bashan may have to go back on his word to burn some of the dead bodies. It has been almost five months since Mansour along with his wife Zebbal has reign into power over the people of the valley of Bashan though it looked as if everyone wills live peacefully soon there will be a few people, who will become sick with fever as well as blood, red pot marks all over their body and those victims of those pot marks will burn with fever, even though his queen Zebbal has been instrumental in placing women from both tribes to look after the sick in a different area far from the commune where Zebbal lives with her husband Mansour, and the other people of the valley of the giants.

“Tell them to get out of the waters, or they will poison the water,” Mansour says even though by now some of the cattle of Bashan has died, and land in the valley looks to a little parched even though there is still a few vineyards budding out plump, grapes. Mansour somewhat knows of the condensation knew as rain maybe falling down soon, for the now monarch of the valley of Bashan has seen his share of the famines, and now Mansour do not believe if he could be able to guide the people if another famine happens, yet he knows he cannot cower down because Mansour it looks has fought to death for his future title also for his wife aka queen Zebbal.

“One of our crafts persons, have made a cart. I will go, and find other men to help place those people in the cart and carry them to the area," the man says right now Mansour knows of the area the man is referring. Motioning the man to go to take care of the people, who are wadding the lakes around the valley of Bashan obviously trying to ease their pains from the sores on their bodies, while inside his new house the one built for he, and Zebbal a much bigger one like a stony, like palace, the leader of both tribes of Bashan will come to a conclusion inside of his head. If a certain number of the people die from whatever has come over the valley of the giants, then Mansour the general turned leader will set up a funeral pyre like to burn those bodies. Mansour will not believe of what is happening in the valley is a result of maybe a curse from either of the gods of Bashan or one placed on the valley of Bashan from the now dead, high priest Bahina. At the moment, Mansour will stand up from his thorn likes structure build by the men, who has rebuilt the stony, palace like building for Mansour now he will walk outside to see some of the Bashanite are outside standing on thin like limbs trying to steady their bodies those covered with the reddish, pot marks. As he listens to the moans, and groans from the afflicted all a sudden one woman of the lofty men one name Liah will approach Mansour, her at one time beautiful face covered with the reddish marks, and the sores are easing with the sickening like pulse.

"YOU BROUGHT THIS EVIL UPON US. THE GODS ARE PUNISHING US FOR THE DEATH OF THE HIGH PRIEST BASHAN," the afflicted Liah says all a sudden she charges straight at Mansour her nails out to claw the general now king of the valley of Bashan if the sickening woman is able to do, yet before she comes close to Mansour he will push her back with his sword right now Liah falls down on the ground and it looks as if her breath is leaving her frail, body covered with the reddish, pot marks.

“Take her away,” Mansour says as two men run to where he is standing outside his stony, carved palace like home and the afflicted Liah is on the ground. As the two men lift her body, right now Mansour's wife will run to him and she only looks as the two men are carting away the sick, Bashanite woman Liah.

“There is more sick people,” Zebbal says right now Mansour despite his personal objections will at the moment explains to Zebbal if those sick people dies, then a funeral pyre must be made to burn the bodies and not to the false gods of the valley of Bashan. Ever since Mansour, and Zebbal are now the new monarchs of the valley the temples of the sun god, and the Moon goddess is slowly crashing down also on those stony like altars inside of both temples vines, and weeds are growing showing more neglect to the two temples. After she agrees with her husband to return to the certain section of the valley of where the sick are indeed dying all of a sudden rain will begin to fall and although the rain is no use in easing the people of the valley of the giants any relief it is what happens as the rains continue to fall. With some of the more well people of the valley scrambling to their homes all of a sudden the rains from the skies above Bashan is falling more heavily next lightning will fill the skies covered now with thick, billowy clouds almost blocking out the sun. Having the one instinct to go to his wife, as the rains fall more and more with each drop likes a thick, watery sheet as Mansour hurries to the other end of the hectare of the valley of where the sick of Bashan is the general Mansour will take note the lakes are filling up too fast and the dirt likes pavements of the valley is slowly turning into sloshes of mud.

“MANSOUR, WHAT ARE WE TO DO?” A man shouts out to Mansour as he is running to catch up with the general. With rain dripping from his face, and wetting up his fur likes clothes and his hair right now Mansour will tell the man to have the people of the valley if they are able to run to the hilly region of where the giants lives. Running along now to tell the tribes if they are able to do as what Mansour has instructed the more the general runs to the region of the valley of where the sick are housed, the rains from the skies above the valley of Bashan are becoming darker also more rains are falling coming down more heavily like having a watery shield as if the tribes of the valley of the giants cannot see right in front of their scared like faces. "MY HUSBAND, WHAT IS HAPPENING?" Zebbal shouts out as she runs, and met up with Mansour the falling rains almost blinds Zebbal to the point she cannot in plain sight sees in front of her.

"I do not know. You, and I must go to the hilly region of the giants," Mansour says even though he trusts the man, he had told about the other people of the valley to run to the hilly region the ones not too sick will obeys the general Mansour. At the moment, the more the rains fall from out of the clouds the more it becomes difficult for the two tribes of the valley to run up the hilly region as the ones, who are able to run are now slipping further, and further downhill like as the rains come down now in thick, watery sheets blinding the few cattle still alive as well as the two tribes, in the valley of Bashan. During the harrowing moment, the three giants one now dead still on the ground the one Arek since the disease has come down on his body, but the other colossal name Jabesh is trying to run up an even higher mountain in the hilly region as the rains come down more, and harder the colossal will find his bulky like body slipping also his feet slipping as Jabesh is trying to climb the highest mountain of Bashan, but it will be to no avail because the rains are not only coming down with a fierceness the lakes in the valley of Bashan also in the hilly region of the giants are filling to capacity having soon the entire valley of Bashan to overflow with water. As the waters rise higher, and higher also as Mansour is holding onto Zebbal he is also trying his best not to have her to look behind her as Mansour, and his wife is trying to reach dry and higher land. As the two is walking, and sliding up the hilly region of the plains of the giants it seems as if the more Mansour, and Zebbal keeps climbing their feet are becoming bogged in the mud of the hills and now what will frighten even Mansour with his wife the trees, and vegetation of the hills, and valley are now washed away as the rains pour down heavier from the skies the thunder keeps reverberating as the rains continue to fall. As the two is trying not to look at the bodies drowning in the flood of waters also the cattle bleating while trying to keep their meat heads above the rising tides of water the more the rains fall from the skies above the valley of Bashan, the deeper and more watery like shields the rains will make. In a moment, Mansour will lose his grip on his wife Zebbal as she screams out to her husband, in a flash of the time of the deluge, the general will try to swim back to rescue Zebbal now it is too late as the flood waters rising higher, and higher is carrying her body away with a full, watery force away. Screaming up at the skies above the hilly region of Bashan as he is trying to swim in the water, and heavily downslides of the mud the general Mansour will realize his strength his not match for the down pour of the rains from the skies above Bashan. Losing more of his strength, the general Mansour will stop his swimming to save himself from the high rising, flood waters as he drowns along with all of the people of Bashan before the flood waters recede there will not be one living soul left in the entire valley.

As for the giants, who lives in the hilly region of Bashan, as the flood waters to rise higher and higher, the dead and decaying body of the lofty name Arek will be washed away pushing, and bumping into the smaller dead ones of the valley as they all float away. The one giant name Jabesh after running, and sliding up the mountain sensing he is now safe will suddenly feel the mountain he is standing on slip and slid in a muddy like way as the rain continues to come down more covering the hills, and the valley of Bashan having the region appearing like one huge bowl of water. However, the colossal Jabesh will keep trying to reach the very top of the mountain evens though the rains will keep pouring down it seems more than the condensation had started as the giant Jabesh was making his way to the mountain to safety, while standing ever so still at the very top of the mountain looking down at the giant Arek floating away with the two tribes of the valley of Bashan everyone dead from the drowning, Jabesh's hair is mop of wet water as he tries to look all around him, at the moment he will sense his body is slowly sliding down from the mountain in a tidal, wave flood of water as the rains come down so fiercely the skies above the hilly region as well as the valley of Bashan is covered out by the rising flood waters. As he tries to cling to the mountain the fractal of the mountain is not high enough to save Jabesh as the lofty giant's colossal like body begins to first become submerged in the mudslides of the mountain until Jabesh is covered in the wet mud also he is suffocating more as the rains fall on, and on as the entire earth becomes submerged by the deluge, in the valley of the giants as well as Bashan there will not be one living soul because all will be drowned out carcasses as the rains will slowly recedes within days.

Another lofty while still inside of his cavern, was starving his body in grief when the deluge happened in the hills also the valley of Bashan. As the flood waters become higher, and higher the lofty man Kalev will open his eyes slowly to a watery tomb as his cavern will fill up so fast, and even if he could; Kalev did not stand one chance of crawling out of his cavern. Because of the flood tides from the heavy rains, his body now dead will float out of his cavern and the inside of Kalev's hiding place will cave in by the heavy rains, now his body barely visible will float away among the other dead of the hills and valley of Bashan. Higher, and higher the waters will keep swelling until not even the highest mountain in Bashan could be seen ever again. When after a certain number of days as the flood waters are receding, there is the dead of the hills, and the valley of Bashan as well as the entire world. The few cattle still left in Bashan will be nothing except bloated, diseased like carcass not even fit for the vultures to eat whenever the entire earth as well as the hills and valley of Bashan become drier. As each, and every day passes, the flood waters will recede and clouds will slowly move away having the bright sunshine to filter through the clouds and because of the deluge, there has never been such a silence likes the valley of Bashan a place where infamous, and towering men had lived among a group of people, who feared and revered the giants like gods. Days of the earth finally is dried all the way, the valley of Bashan now is covered with bloated, drowned out bodes and their homes are now flatten out by the heavy downpour of rains, the two temples once stood in the valley of Bashan one of the temples are now a flat out mud base, the other one used to worship the Moon goddess of the people of Bashan still stands somewhat with only two of the temple's wall are down, yet inside of the Moon goddess's temple is the blank, out face shaped like the Moon supposedly it's grim like grin staring down at the once, bloodied up altar as if the fake deity is laughing at the destruction of the valley of Bashan by powerful, flood waters from the heavens of where the symbol of the Moon goddess the celestial one known as the Moon is continues to wax, and wan despite the deluge.

www.ingramcontent.com/pod-product-compliance
Lightning Source LLC
LaVergne TN
LVHW010618100826
845148LV00014B/3024

* 9 7 8 0 6 1 5 9 0 0 5 6 8 *